PALE PHOENIX

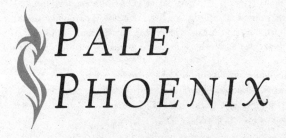

PALE
PHOENIX

Kathryn Reiss

Harcourt Brace & Company

San Diego   New York   London

Requests for permission to make copies of any part of
the work should be mailed to: Permissions Department,
Harcourt Brace & Company, 6277 Sea Harbor Drive,
Orlando, Florida 32887–6777.

Library of Congress Cataloging-in-Publication Data
Reiss, Kathryn.
Pale phoenix/Kathryn Reiss.—1st ed.
p. cm.
Summary: When her parents take in a strange orphan girl with a
mysterious past, fifteen-year-old Miranda decides to find out why
she seems to have come from nowhere and how she seems to be
able to disappear at will.
ISBN 0-15-200030-5
[1. Supernatural—Fiction.   2. Time travel—Fiction.]   I. Title.
PZ7.R2776Pal 1994
[Fic]—dc20   93-32299

Designed by Lydia D'moch
Printed in Hong Kong

First edition
ABCDE

For Kathryn Grace Sawyer—
my oldest friend in the world

*With special thanks to my agent
and longtime supporter,*
Marilyn Marlow

*This book was written
with the aid of a grant from the*
New Jersey State Council on the Arts.

"So the blessed Phoenix, his death-hour over,
His dear old home once again seeketh. . . ."

—*"The Phoenix"*
From the 8th-century Anglo-Saxon poem
attributed to Cynewulf, translated by
J. Lesslie Hall, 1902

"And to die is different from what any one
supposed, and luckier. . . ."

—*Walt Whitman,*
"Song of Myself"

CHAPTER ONE

ON THE MORNING it all began, Miranda Browne had no idea this day would be different from others. Only afterward, looking back, it seemed there had been signs. The cold morning late in January dawned as though a dream, white and heavy with blankets of snow, with thick, white flakes still falling past her window. Silence enfolded the house as Miranda lay warm and snug beneath her quilt, listening for the usual morning sounds. But there was no grind of snowplows or cars going by on the road, no drone overhead of airplanes on their way to the Boston airport, not even the usual beat from the radio down in the kitchen. The whole world might have been catapulted back to an earlier time, when mornings always broke this way: fresh, bright, and soundless.

Wincing as her bare feet touched the cold wooden floor, Miranda crossed to her window seat and rubbed a clear patch on the frosted pane. New-fallen snow blanketed the shrubs, the fences, Dan's house across the street. The magnolia tree outside Miranda's window sparkled in the gray morning sun, its snow-laden branches dripping with ice ornaments. For a moment the scene outside appeared to her as if it were an old photograph in a museum exhibit—a winter morning frozen forever in black and white.

Later, looking back, Miranda decided the silence that morning had been a sign, as loud in its own way as a warning bell. *Something is going to happen*, it tolled.

And something did.

Miranda dressed quickly in jeans, a warm sweater, and thick socks. She yanked a brush through her tangled dark curls and hurried out into the chilly hallway and down the stairs to the kitchen. "Hi, you guys. Did you listen to the radio?"

"School's open, believe it or not," her father, Philip, greeted her. He was sitting at the kitchen table reading the newspaper. "I don't know how the buses are going to get out in all this, but the newspaper was right on time, so maybe it isn't as bad down in town as it looks up here."

"I'll die if people can't get out to come to the flea market," moaned Miranda. "After all our work!" She pulled out her chair and sat down.

Her parents sat watching the flakes fall outside the window over the sink. Helen, Miranda's mother, held a mug of strong black coffee. Her china plate was laden with two buttered bran muffins. Philip sipped a glass of frothy pink milk—his usual diet drink. There was no plate at his place, but he had finally moved beyond the days of eyeing Miranda's and Helen's food jealously. Since losing nearly one hundred pounds, Philip Browne was a man of new energy and drive.

Now he drained his glass and carried it to the dishwasher. "I'm off," he said. "That is, I hope to be off, if the roads aren't too bad. But at least the snow is beautiful here."

"Quite a change from New York," Helen agreed.

Miranda nodded and bit eagerly into a warm muffin. Garnet snow was crisp and white and sparkling, unlike the snow in New York City, which grew gray as soon as it touched the streets. The Brownes had moved to Massachusetts from New York two years ago when Miranda was thirteen, leaving their cramped city apartment for this spacious old home in a small town near Boston.

"I'm driving you to school today," Helen told Miranda, clearing the table. "And Dan, too, if he's ready to go in fifteen minutes." Miranda's mother had a private gynecological and obstetric practice in the Garnet town center and spent hours each week at the Garnet Hospital as well, delivering her patients' babies. "Let's get all these bags of junk out to the car now."

"Mither!" The affectionate nickname Miranda used for her mother came out as a screech. "Mither, that's *perfectly* fine stuff." She glanced at the brown grocery bags crowding the corner behind the door. "We're not supposed to sell anything that isn't in good condition."

"All I know is that I'm delighted to get it out of the house." Helen smiled. "I can't believe we've collected so much rubbish over the years."

"What I can't believe," Philip put in, as he wound his scarf around his coat collar, "is that you insisted on lugging all of it here from New York in the first place." He shook his head. "You pack rat!"

Helen came to kiss him at the back door. Philip waved good-bye and headed through the unshoveled drifts behind their house toward the old barn that now served as a garage. He had given up a career as a professor of American History at the City College when they moved to Garnet. Now he was an assistant curator and research director at the American Museum in Lexington. He said he had burned out as a teacher. Students studied history only for the credit toward graduation, he felt; they didn't have any love of the past at all. At least museum visitors came out of a genuine interest in America's history.

"I bet we sell everything," predicted Miranda as her mother swept out the snow that flew in when Philip left. "It seems everybody's interested in the Witch House now."

The Witch House was the old Prindle House, Garnet's oldest building. It was nicknamed for Nathaniel Prindle, who had been an avid witch-hunter back in the days when people's fear of witches erupted into hysteria. He built the house for his family in 1692, and generations of Prindles lived there until the family eventually died out and the house was bought by the town. It had served as a hospital, a village school, an orphanage, and a library before being abandoned, too run-down for public use.

Eventually the house grew so derelict, the city planned to demolish it and build a new community center on the same site, with the empty yard next door made into a parking lot. Garnet folklore long held that the yard was haunted by one of the poor souls Mr. Prindle had accused of witchcraft. On a windy day, legend had it, you could hear wails of anguish.

The local Historical Society stepped in and clamored for the Prindle House to be saved. Eventually the townspeople voted for the old house to be renovated into the much-needed community center. And the high school was helping by holding fund-raisers—a Halloween haunted house in the school gym had been the first of these. Now the flea market promised to draw a crowd, and a dance was in the works.

Miranda stood up, cramming a last piece of muffin into her mouth. "I'd better go call Dan," she mumbled. "You know he's probably still asleep." She went to the phone, picturing his tousled dark hair and sleepy eyes.

"Tell him ten minutes," said Helen. "If I can get my car started."

On the way to school, Dan Hooton rummaged through the cardboard box he had stowed in the car and pulled out a pink china piggy bank.

"Look at this. Ugly as sin, but I bet we can get ten bucks for it."

"If not, your parents can start a 'Garnet Kitsch' exhibit," teased Miranda. The Hootons' large pre-Revolutionary War home housed the Garnet Museum in one wing. Dan's parents ran the township museum themselves, collecting memorabilia of Garnet history for the displays. Miranda's father maintained that he owed his present job in Lexington to Ed Hooton, who had first introduced him to the curator of the American Museum.

"Who would buy it?" Miranda wondered, examining the pink pig as Helen drove slowly down the hill. "It's too pink." She handed it back to Dan. "I've got two teddy bears, some dominoes, a clock radio, and loads of old camping gear."

"Pretty cool," said Dan, rummaging around in his box. "I've got a bunch of old books and coffee mugs. And this. It's a whistle." He held up a small white stone figure and put it to his lips. A clear, high note piped loud and true as Helen piloted the car through the Garnet center. The road wound around the old village common and it was just there, where the road curved, that a girl stepped suddenly off the sidewalk, straight into the path of their car.

The long note from Dan's whistle still hung in the air as Helen slammed on the brakes and jerked the steering wheel to the left. The car swerved and skidded off the road into a snowbank. The girl lay motionless in the street.

"Oh, my God!" Helen jumped from the car and rushed to the fallen figure. Miranda wrestled with her seatbelt, her breakfast muffins now a hard mass in her stomach.

Miranda and Dan knelt in the street while Helen tried to revive the girl. A small crowd began to gather, and several cars slid slowly to a stop behind them. Miranda's first thought as she gazed down on the girl was that she must be dead. She blended too well with the fresh, soft snow to have warm blood pumping in her veins. Her long hair, wispy and pale, lay fanned out around her body. She lay utterly still, her thin coat of dirty beige wool covered with a light sprinkling of snow.

A very large beaded satchel had fallen in the snow next to the girl. Miranda had never seen anything quite like it. Shaped like an old-fashioned carpet bag, it was covered in gaudy pink beads. Some of the beads had a silvery cast, and in several places swatches of faded cloth showed through. Notebooks and pens had spilled out of the beaded bag and now dotted the street like dark smudges next to the unmoving girl. Feeling helpless, Miranda began gathering the things up.

A blue vein throbbed on the girl's neck, and her eyes slowly opened. They, too, were strangely pale, a funny milky beige that nearly matched her colorless hair. She focused on Miranda. "Don't touch those things—" Her voice was small and frightened. Slowly she sat up with Helen's support.

Miranda realized only then that she had been holding her breath, and she let it out in a puff of frosty cloud. She set the beaded satchel in the snow next to the girl. "I was just—"

"Did you take anything?" asked the girl, reaching for the bag.

"Wait, don't move," cautioned Helen. "You may have broken something."

"I'm all right," said the girl. She slanted a glance up at Helen. "Don't worry about me."

"Cracked a rib, maybe," said an elderly man who had stopped to see what had happened. "Girl ought to have a doctor look at her."

"I am a doctor." Helen bent lower to examine the girl, feeling her gently through the thin coat for signs of injury. Then she put her arms around the girl to help her to her feet. "Are you sure you can stand?"

"I'm fine. I said I was all right." The girl

pulled away and reached down for her satchel. Miranda frowned at her.

"What's your name, dear? I'm Helen Browne. Where are you going? Let me drive you there." Helen's voice was worried.

"I'm going to school. To the high school." She brushed snow off her coat with a flutter of thin fingers. "But I can walk."

"We're on our way there, too," said Dan.

"I *said* I can walk."

"I still say a doctor should see to her," spoke up the old man. "Get an X-ray."

"Listen, I'm really fine. The car never touched me. I just wasn't watching where I was going and—I just slipped. That's all. I'm sorry I made you run off the road. I hope you can get your car out of the snowbank." This was all said in a rapid monotone, and Miranda shivered despite her warm red jacket and scarf. The girl sounded so odd—like a recording of a girl. As if she weren't really there at all and only her voice were talking. . . .

The girl turned away and walked carefully back to the sidewalk. "Thank you, all of you. I'm sorry to worry you. I really am . . . quite fine." Most of the people who had gathered began to leave now that they realized the girl was not injured.

Helen lifted her gloved hands helplessly. Miranda sighed with relief. "I guess there's nothing we can do," she told her mother. "If she says she doesn't need help, then I guess she doesn't." They all watched the girl moving slowly down the slippery sidewalk.

"She looks 'quite fine' to me," said Dan. "Weird, but all in one piece."

"Looks like you're the ones needing help." Two men who had been part of the crowd moved to the car in the snowbank. "Let's see if we can get you on your way again."

"Oh, thank you," said Helen, turning back to the car. They all began the business of tugging it out of the snow. Helen kept looking over her shoulder. "I don't feel right about letting her go." The car slid backward out of the drift.

"Maybe you two can keep an eye on her at school today," one of the men suggested to Miranda and Dan.

"What did she say her name was?" asked Helen.

"She didn't," said Miranda.

At two o'clock the high school students began setting up their wares in the gymnasium. Banners painted with slogans hung across the room:

Save the Witch House! and **What Would We Do** *Witchout* **the Prindle House?!** By three o'clock the first customers filtered in, many with small children in tow. Miranda moved the two stuffed bears to the front of her display. "These should catch their eyes," she murmured to her friend Susannah. "It's just a matter of knowing the customer."

Susannah sighed. "Well, I know no customer's going to want these old jigsaw puzzles. And my mother refuses to let them back into the house. We already have dozens. My dad is addicted. Do you think I can *give* them away?"

"Sure. Buy a stuffed bear, get a free puzzle." Miranda cast her eyes across the crowded gymnasium, searching for Dan. Her gaze rested suddenly on the small, white face and pale, long hair of the girl who had fallen in the street. Miranda turned to Susannah. "Listen, can you handle all my stuff as well as your own for a few minutes? Try to get those little boys over here to buy the bears. Tell them it's a great deal at only three dollars per bear. I'll be right back."

She pressed through the throng of people, stepping adroitly around display tables jumbled with castoffs. When she came upon the girl, she stopped. "Hi. I saw you—and just had to come ask, well, you know. Whether you're really okay. After this morning."

The girl sat hunched at a regular classroom desk. Some pieces of jewelry, several tools, a fine silk scarf, and a lot of silverware in need of polishing lay before her. The girl's pale eyes flickered to Miranda's face, then away. "I told you I was fine."

Miranda hesitated. "I'm Miranda Browne." She waited, but the girl was looking down at the jewelry, fingering one of the rings. "Well, what's your name?"

Again the eyes flickered. "Look, do you want to buy something?"

"No. I just wanted—"

"Why not?" The girl shook her pale hair back over her shoulders. "The jewelry is real, you know. I bet your mother would like it."

"She doesn't wear much jewelry, and I only have ten bucks anyway." Miranda frowned. "What's your name?" she asked again. "You're new here, right? I haven't seen you around."

The girl rearranged the items in her meager display. "I really need to sell this stuff."

Miranda shook her head, exasperated. Apparently the girl was going to guard the secret of her name as if it were some precious jewel. "Well, it looks like good stuff. I'm sure you'll sell some of it, and it ought to bring in a lot of money for the Prindle House."

"Oh, yes, that's right. We do have to take

care of our past, don't we?" The girl's voice was expressionless.

Dan was right; the girl was weird. "I think it's important to try." Miranda's voice was sharp. "Don't you?"

"Look, my name is Abby," the girl offered suddenly. Her voice sounded choked. "And if you aren't going to buy anything, then maybe you'll move on and give other people the chance to look. I really need to sell this stuff."

Miranda stared at her, taken aback. "Well, *excuse* me!"

The girl looked about ready to burst into tears. But Miranda didn't want to stay and find out what the problem was. She looked around the crowded room and saw Dan tending his table in the eleventh grade section. She hurried toward him gratefully, nearly knocking over a card table in her haste to cross the gym.

He threw his arm around her shoulders in welcome, another of the new affectionate gestures he had been making the last few weeks. It was a casual enough move, but it made Miranda worry. She and Dan had been close friends from the day they'd met. She liked him so much, she didn't want any of the usual boy-girl complications wrecking their friendship. So she gently moved out of the circle of his arm as she spoke: "I just saw Abby, and boy, you sure were right when you said she was weird."

He put his hands into his pockets. "Who's Abby?"

"The girl we hit this morning. The one we *didn't* hit."

"Well, is she all right?"

"She said she was." Miranda shrugged. "But she was totally rude about it."

"Oh, well, at least you can tell your mom you talked to her and she's not dead. Right?" He steered her closer to his table. "Now, Ms. Browne. Look at all this great museum-quality stuff. Tell me you can resist any of it."

Miranda laughed. "I can resist all of it."

"What about the pink pig? Remember—every cent goes to the Prindle House fund."

"I'm afraid I can resist it, even then."

"Can you resist me?"

A warm flush crept up Miranda's cheeks. She did not answer, but snatched off his table the first item that came to hand. "So, how much is this whistle, then?" It was the one he had blown in the car that morning.

"You can have it. A gift." His voice was huskier than usual.

"No, I really should donate some money to our cause." She inspected the little statue so she wouldn't have to look at him. She wished they could just act natural with each other.

The whistle was a bird about three inches high, carved out of cold, white stone. The bottom of the base was covered in a circle of green felt. The statue was smoothly and intricately detailed, with small feathered wings and a sharp beak. The bird resembled an eagle, but its folded wings were longer, its face faintly human. It seemed to smile.

"It's a stone phoenix," Dan told her.

"What's that?"

"It's the bird from the legend. You know— about the bird who rises out of its own funeral pyre to live again and again."

She noticed gratefully that his voice was back to normal. "Sounds bizarre."

"Yeah. I don't really know much about it. My mom found it in a jumble of stuff that was donated to the museum. She knows the whole legend. Get her to tell you." He moved away to wait on a teacher, who wanted to know the price of a pair of wooden candlesticks.

Miranda turned the stone figure over and over in her hand. She found it strangely fascinating. She raised it to her lips and blew into the small hole at the top of its head. Across the gymnasium she saw Abby raise her head and look around, startled at the high, clear note.

Miranda waited while Dan sold the candlesticks. She waited while he sold the ugly china pig to Mrs. Wainwright, who was his great-aunt and Miranda's flute teacher. Mrs. Wainwright claimed she wanted it for her collection of china animals that sat atop the grand piano. When she walked away, carrying her pig, Dan turned back to Miranda, grinning. "See? See? Ten bucks."

Miranda snorted. "She took pity on you, that's what I see."

"Hey, you'd better get back," he said suddenly. "Susannah's going crazy over there."

Miranda glanced at her friend, who was beckoning her. Their table was crowded with customers. She held out the stone whistle to Dan. "I really do want this," she said. "How much is it?"

"Well, if I can get ten bucks for my beautiful pig, I have to ask as much for such a rare old bird."

Miranda thought ten dollars was a bit steep for such a little bit of stone, but she handed him her only bill readily enough, telling herself the money was for the Prindle House. Dan stuffed the money into a jar.

She felt him watching her as she hurried

over to Susannah. Two small boys were clamoring for the bears; a woman was eager to purchase the dominoes and was waving her checkbook over the heads of the other customers. The old man who had stopped when Abby fell in the road was interested in the camping stove. He recognized Miranda and smiled.

As Miranda took her place behind the table and smiled back, she found her gaze moving beyond him, across the room to Abby at her little desk. A tremor went through her, and she reached her hand back to touch the chill of the stone whistle in her jeans pocket. Unaccountably she felt a sense of great loss, almost a feeling of homesickness, steal over her. It was ridiculous, of course, for here she was in her own school, classmates all around her, and Susannah and Dan, her mother only blocks away in her office, her father maybe already on his way back from Lexington. But Miranda wanted to be home, *needed* to be home, cozily ensconced in her window seat with a book, with her parents down in the kitchen at the table drinking tea and a fire crackling in the living room grate. Why did the gym seem suddenly so barren and cold? As she pressed a free jigsaw puzzle on the old man, a vision flickered briefly across the back of her mind: Abby lying so still in the snow, those pale eyes meeting her own.

CHAPTER TWO

ALTHOUGH MIRANDA RESOLVED to forget about Abby, she found herself thinking about the girl all afternoon. She quizzed Susannah about her, but learned only that Abby's last name was Chandler, and that she was new in Susannah's science class. A boy who was browsing at their table and actually bought one of the jigsaw puzzles overheard and said Abby Chandler had moved to Garnet only a couple of weeks ago. Even though she looked too young for tenth grade, she was in his homeroom. He told them she kept to herself. Miranda asked other kids who came to their table, but no one knew anything more about Abby.

In the car on the way home, Miranda told her mother she had tried her best to talk to the girl. Dan sat in the backseat but leaned forward to add that Abby didn't seem injured.

Helen sighed, driving carefully through the snow-covered lanes. "I thought about the poor thing all day. Even if she says she wasn't hurt, it still was a nasty fall. And so sudden—it almost seemed a faint. She was awfully pale, didn't you think? And so thin. I'm worried about her."

"I get the feeling she doesn't want us bothering her, Mither."

"Well, I feel responsible. I'm going to call her parents."

"I hope they aren't as rude as she is."

"Oh, Mandy, she's probably just lonely. It's hard being the new kid at school."

"I know all about being the new girl, don't forget. But in order to make friends, you have to be friendly. It isn't as if I didn't even try, Mither. She was totally weird when I talked to her. No *wonder* she doesn't have any friends."

"It's not like you to be so uncharitable." Helen glanced over at Miranda sharply. "Don't be so quick to judge."

"I don't know what it is. I just don't like her." She felt the pressure of Dan's hand on her shoulder and pressed her lips together, scowling out the window. Dusk came early now, and already the windows of the houses they passed were filled with warm yellow light. From the backseat, Dan reached forward and gently tugged a strand of her hair.

Helen slid the car to a stop in front of the Hootons' house. Miranda got out of the front seat so Dan could climb out. Virginia Hooton, Dan's mother, threw aside a snow shovel and struggled through the drifts in the driveway to their car. Helen rolled down the window.

"Hi." Mrs. Hooton smiled, bending down to peer in the window at Helen. "Slippery enough for you?"

Helen grimaced. "Cold enough, too. I wonder if I'll even be able to get in our driveway."

"How did the flea market go?" asked Mrs. Hooton. "I stopped by, but I couldn't stay. I had to get back to the Prindle House. We're setting up an exhibit about the history of the house to help with fund-raising. It's hard work."

"Poor Mom," said Dan, clapping her on the shoulder with a handful of snow.

"Keep away from me with that white stuff," she warned him. "Or you'll get a whole drift of it packed into your shirt."

"See how she treats me?" Dan appealed to Miranda. "Can I come live with you instead?"

Miranda grinned at him but spoke to his

mother. "The place was a mob scene." She reached into her coat pocket and drew out the stone whistle. "I bought this."

"Oh, the phoenix. How much did he charge you for it?"

"Ten dollars."

"Hmm." Virginia Hooton glanced at her son. "I doubt it's worth that much—though maybe I'm wrong. It does look quite old. It was in a box of junk I got at an estate sale when old Mrs. Penny died. The box had been up in her attic for ages, unopened. It was labeled 'From Uncle Henry Longridge, Boston.' Whoever that was, I don't know. But since it wasn't Garnet history, it doesn't belong in our museum."

Miranda lifted the bird to her lips and blew its single note into the air. Then she shivered as the wind picked up and rattled the brown leaves left in the elm trees in Dan's front yard.

"It's an interesting legend." Mrs. Hooton clapped her gloved hands together to warm them. "When the phoenix had lived five hundred years, its time came to die. So it would build a fire and throw itself into the flames. I wouldn't mind some nice warm flames myself just now!"

"You mean it committed suicide?" asked Miranda.

"Oh, no—it was a way of living forever. When the fire burned out, there would be a small new phoenix born out of the ashes—and the whole cycle would begin again. It's a comforting thought, really."

"Too bad we can't do that," said Dan.

"Oh, I don't know," mused Helen from inside the car. "I think you might get tired of it after awhile. I know I wouldn't really want to be a kid over and over."

Mrs. Hooton laughed. "True enough. I'd especially hate to be a teenager again. All those raging hormones."

"Oh, great," muttered Dan. "Thanks a lot, Mom."

Virginia Hooton looped an arm around his waist and stepped away from the car. "You must be cold sitting there with the window open, Helen. And we have shoveling to do. See you later."

"Did I hear you say *we* have shoveling to do?" Miranda heard Dan moan as they drove slowly up the hill of their own driveway. Miranda turned to wave at him out the rear window.

She followed her mother into the house. Philip strode down the stairs to greet his wife and daughter as they entered the front hall, his long legs taking the steps three at a time. "My ladies! At last! I've been home more than an hour, worrying you were stuck in a drift somewhere."

"We were this morning," Helen told him, shrugging out of her coat and sniffing appreciatively. "What's for dinner?"

"Vegetable soup," he said. "With lots of noodles for the two of you, and lots of plain broth for me. Hot soup seemed right for a day like this."

"I'll let you sniff my noodles," teased Helen. She was proud of her husband's firm resolve where his diet was concerned.

"Look, it's snowing again," said Miranda, following the smell of fragrant soup into the kitchen. She left her parents exchanging a long kiss in the hallway. It always made her feel warm and happy to see them so affectionate and loving. She took three mugs out of the cupboard next to the sink and three packets of instant hot chocolate from the box in the pantry. "No Fat, No Sugar" the label promised. Even her father could drink this stuff. She poured water into the mugs and popped them into the microwave.

"How did the flea market go?" Philip asked when he and Helen joined Miranda in the kitchen.

"Well, we sold a lot," Miranda told him,

leaning against the counter. "I don't know what the final total is yet—but I bet there'll be buckets of money for the Prindle House. There were even more people there today than at our haunted house." She looked out at the thick snowflakes falling past the window and remembered their most successful fund-raiser to date, the Halloween haunted house in the gym. She and Susannah had dressed as witches and sold candy apples.

"So what's this about landing in a snowbank?" Philip asked Helen.

"I almost hit a girl," she told him, and launched into the whole story of their morning ride to school. "I'm dying to call her parents now to check up on her," she finished. "I've been worrying all day."

He handed her the phone directory. "Good idea."

"What was her last name, Mandy?" asked Helen, opening the book.

"Chandler." Miranda frowned at her mother. She wished Helen would stop carrying on about the weird girl. The microwave timer buzzed, and Miranda opened the door. She handed her parents their mugs of cocoa.

Helen set her mug on the table as she flipped through the phone book. "Chan—, Chandler, here we go. There's only one in the book, so that makes it easy." She reached for the phone and pressed the numbers. Miranda sipped her cocoa and listened.

"Hello?" Helen's voice was suddenly the one Miranda called her "doctor voice," smoothly professional, utterly competent. "This is Dr. Helen Browne. I'm calling about your daughter, Abby. . . . Oh? Really?" Helen's voice faltered. "Then, excuse me. I thought—no. I guess I have the wrong number. Sorry to bother you." She replaced the receiver.

"Abby doesn't live there?" asked Philip.

"The man said he lives alone and doesn't have any children. But that's the only Chandler in the book."

"Oh, Mither, so what?" Miranda took her empty mug to the sink and turned the water on hard. "Maybe they have an unlisted number. Or maybe since they only moved here a couple of weeks ago they're not in the book—try information. Or maybe Abby's mother has remarried and the phone is listed under a different name. Or maybe—maybe anything!" She didn't understand why she felt so annoyed.

"You're right, of course," said Helen. "But I feel bad about it. The poor girl looked so lost, so weak. . . ."

Miranda turned off the water and moved to

the stove. She stirred the big pot of vegetable soup, unaccountably restless and irritable. "Look, I have homework," she said abruptly. "Will you call me when the soup's ready?"

Miranda hurried out of the kitchen, then up the stairs to her bedroom. She threw herself onto the bed. Why was she so unhappy? Feeling something hard under her hip, she reached into her pocket and tugged the stone phoenix out.

She raised it to her lips and blew the single sweet note. As it died away, she heard her parents' laughter from downstairs, and the same tremor of homesickness and loss that assailed her at school stabbed at her again. What was wrong with her? Dragging herself off the bed, she crossed the room to the dresser, opened her sock drawer, and dropped the phoenix in.

At lunchtime the next day, Miranda walked with Susannah to the cafeteria. Her friend was flushed with excitement. "Can you believe it? Over five thousand dollars in one day!"

"It's a good start," Miranda agreed. But she knew it would cost hundreds of thousands of dollars to turn the derelict Witch House into a community center. Still, their school's contribution brought the house a small step closer to its new life.

"And next—the dance." Susannah twirled

as they entered the cafeteria, her blond curls dancing. "Shall we go together, or ask guys?"

"Oh—let's just go as a group. It's easier." Miranda's mind wasn't on the Valentine's Dance, scheduled for the next weekend. She saw Abby up ahead. The thin, flaxen-haired girl was wrapped in her dirty beige coat as if she were cold, and she moved slowly, eyeing the selections. "Wait a sec," Miranda said to Susannah. "I need to ask Abby something."

She pushed through the throng of students waiting for their lunches. "Hi." She stood in line behind Abby.

Abby's colorless eyes looked at her blankly.

"My mother tried to call your parents last night, but we couldn't find your number. It wasn't listed."

"I know." Abby moved forward in line and placed her beaded satchel on the counter. She opened it, glancing furtively over her shoulder at Miranda. The satchel was empty.

"Well, where do you live?"

Abby blinked. "Listen. You tell your mother to stop pestering me. I can get along all right—I mean, I *am* all right."

What did that *mean*, Miranda wondered.

"What'll you have, girls?" The woman behind the counter held up a large spoon. "Mashed potatoes or fries?"

Abby stood motionless for a moment, opened her mouth as if to speak, then closed it. She snapped her beaded bag shut and turned away without ordering anything.

"Next?" inquired the woman.

"Nothing for me, thanks," said Miranda. "I bring my lunch." Perplexed, she looked around for Abby, but didn't see her. She walked back over to Susannah at their usual table in the corner and sat down, greeting the other girls who were there. She scanned the room for Abby and caught sight of Dan at a table on the other side. Then she saw Abby back in line at the lunch counter. *So she decided to eat something after all.*

Abby wasn't pushing a tray along the metal counter. As before, she slid her large beaded satchel along. Then, as if she knew Miranda were watching, Abby turned her back. Miranda forced herself to look away.

The hubbub of all the students grated on Miranda's nerves. Her ears were suddenly extrasensitive to the usual din; she could no longer make out the separate conversations going on at their table, but heard all the voices as a single, throbbing pulse. She pushed away her sandwich and closed her eyes, letting the jarring background tumult wash over her.

After a moment, she opened her eyes,

unwrapped her sandwich, and took a bite, savoring the taste of her mother's special chicken salad and apple filling. Susannah was talking excitedly about the upcoming dance, but Miranda couldn't concentrate. She didn't understand why things seemed wrong. Across the room, Dan was deep in conversation with one of the boys on the debate team. Miranda took another bite, the ringing in her ears subsiding, and noticed Abby making her way swiftly among the tables, heading toward the door to the courtyard. Her beaded satchel, now heavy and bulging, swung against her leg. Miranda put down her sandwich, watching with narrowed eyes.

Abruptly, she left her lunch and books and pressed through the crowded room after Abby. She heard Susannah call to wait, but kept on, determined to confront Abby. About what? She wasn't even sure, but she had a sense that she must follow.

"Hey, Mandy!" Susannah's voice was louder this time. Miranda wheeled around, finger to her lips, and waited for her friend to catch up. Together they paused by the door leading outside into the courtyard.

"Now where'd she go?" asked Miranda, and she hurried outside into the freezing air.

She saw Abby's footprints in the new dusting of snow on the path and followed them.

"Will you tell me what in the world you're doing out here?" cried Susannah. "We're not allowed out here at lunchtime, as you know perfectly well. And it's freezing cold and we don't have our coats, and—"

"Shut up!" Miranda hissed, grabbing her friend's arm and pulling her along. "I've got to see where Abby's going. She's got her bag stuffed with something all of a sudden, and you know what? I think it might be food. I saw her in line and the bag was empty, but now look!" She pointed to where, up ahead, Abby darted out the school gate and crossed Main Street. Her large beaded bag thumped against her side.

"Now it's full," said Susannah. "But so what? Maybe she bought a lot of bags of potato chips or cartons of yogurt or something."

"But she's not allowed to leave school, and yet look at her. She's running away!"

"I don't get you, Mandy," said Susannah, still hurrying along behind her friend as Miranda strode on along the snowy street. "Why risk getting in trouble because Abby's cutting school? What's the big deal?"

Half a block ahead, Abby stopped and turned back as if checking to be sure she was not being followed. "Quick!" Miranda grabbed Susannah's arm and pulled her down behind a snow-topped hedge bordering the schoolyard. "Don't let her see us." Miranda peered around the hedge and watched as Abby slowly turned and trudged down the street. Her head was bent against the wind, the beaded bag slung over one thin shoulder. Miranda pulled Susannah out onto the sidewalk again, and they fell into step a block behind Abby. "Go on back to school if you want," Miranda whispered to Susannah. "But I'm going to see where she's going. I don't know why—but something's really weird about her, and I want to know what it is."

"If you ask me, something's weird about *you*, Mandy!" Susannah, hands on hips, stared at her friend. "I've never seen you acting like this. I *am* going back. Gosh, I never thought I'd be looking forward to geometry, but the classroom is so overheated I might thaw out by the end of the period."

Miranda hardly listened. As Susannah ran back the way they had come, Miranda moved on, following Abby at a distance, passing the little cluster of shops, a dry cleaner, the post office. When Abby stopped again, Miranda darted behind a tree.

Abby peered over her shoulder, then ran across the street and into the corner grocery store. Miranda waited, stamping her feet and rubbing her hands, then blowing on her fingers to warm them. Her teeth were chattering.

Only a few minutes had passed when Abby stepped outside again, her arms full of several loaves of bread and a big jar. She huddled against the wall of the building for only the second it took to stuff the food inside her beige coat and hitch the heavy, beaded satchel onto her shoulder again. Then she sprinted down the first side street.

As Miranda stepped out from her shelter of branches, the store clerk appeared in the doorway across the street. He looked to the left and the right, then saw her. "Hey!" he called. "You see a little girl in a dirty white coat come out? She ripped me off! I can't believe it!"

Miranda crossed the street. "She stole the food?" She wasn't surprised.

"Sure did!" He frowned, hands on hips. "Now, which way did she go?"

The man looked down at the snow and grinned. "Ha! That little sneak won't get far in this snow. I can follow her tracks as easily as if she'd left me a map." He opened the door to the shop and called inside, "Hey, Ralph! Watch the register, will you? I'll be back in a few minutes. Soon as I catch a thief!"

Miranda moved after him down the side

street. Abby's footprints were the only ones in the fresh snow. They were small and narrow compared to Miranda's prints. The man was grumbling as he strode along. "Damn hoodlums. What do they come around here for, anyway? Why can't they stay in the cities?" They rounded the corner, but there was still no sign of Abby.

They pressed on another half a block, but when an icy wind whirled the snow up off the sidewalk, the man stopped and shook his head in disgust. "Damn kids! Damn snow!" he growled. "It's not worth freezing my tail out here." He started stamping back to the corner grocery. Miranda watched him go.

She stood there uncertainly. For a second she wondered what in the world she was doing out in the snow, a mile from school, with no coat or gloves, trailing a girl she didn't even like. But then the moment passed, and she resolutely marched on, following Abby's tracks. At first they were widely spaced, as if Abby had been running. After a block and around a corner they came closer together as if she had slowed to a walk. Miranda scuffed the prints as she walked, obliterating them. And then, around the next corner, she came to an abrupt halt. She sucked in her breath. *What—?*

The footprints were gone. Just like that.

The new-fallen snow on the sidewalk, snow that had been broken only by Abby's small prints and by her own as Miranda tracked her, stretched ahead fresh and unmarred. It was almost, Miranda thought, as if Abby had somehow disappeared into thin air.

What had happened to Abby? Miranda looked all around but could see no sign that Abby had gone into one of the small houses. Could she have climbed up into a tree? Miranda lifted her head to search the bare branches of a towering elm. Nothing. By now she was shivering hard and her hands and feet were numb.

She had come farther than she realized, and it took her nearly twenty minutes to get back to school. As she walked, Miranda was surprised at the blaze of anger she felt toward Abby. The anger warmed her. At last she slipped through the side door of the school and headed for the girls' bathroom. The period was nearly over, and she'd already missed so much of her English class there was little sense in going. She'd have to think of some excuse to give Ms. Taylor.

When the bell rang, Miranda joined the crush of students in the hallway and was borne along to her world history class. She was nearly inside the door, when she felt a hand on her shoulder. "Miranda Browne? Where were you last period?" It was Ms. Taylor, the usually smiling young English teacher.

"I—I was in the bathroom. I felt sick." Miranda, unused to lying, felt her face flush.

"Now, Mandy, I know that isn't true. I sent a student to check the bathrooms. We were searching for you because people had seen you at lunch. If you were sick, you would have gone to the nurse to lie down."

Miranda bowed her head. "I'm sorry. I won't cut again."

"I hope not! This goes on your record, you know. I've already reported it to Mr. Raphael. Cutting once means you have an extra essay to write. Please see me after school to get your assignment."

Miranda said she would and stumbled into the world history classroom. The rest of the afternoon passed in a blur. She heard hardly anything her teachers said. She was humiliated at having been caught and furious at Abby for leading her on such a wild goose chase in the first place. What a creep! Miranda tried not to think about the way those footprints had vanished.

After school she went straight to her locker

to get her coat, books, and flute without waiting for Susannah or Dan. Next she stopped at Ms. Taylor's classroom to write down the extra homework. Then she raced outside into the snow, heading for the little white house on Elm Street where she had a music lesson with Mrs. Wainwright.

Normally Miranda loved her weekly lesson. Eleanor Wainwright, Dan's great-aunt, had become a close and trusted friend of Miranda's the summer the Brownes moved to Garnet. She was getting old, but still had more energy than many younger women. She was spritely and cheerful, always waiting with an after-school snack for her music students and full of questions about their families and friends. She joked that, as President of the Garnet Historical Society, she was just as interested in her students' ancestors as she was in the children themselves. She wore brightly colored silk scarves at her neck and long, dangly earrings. Her music room, too, was ornamented with colors. There were cut flowers in vases, baskets of magazines, miniature collectibles on every bare surface: dolls in international costumes atop the bookcases in the living room, china animals on the piano in the music room.

Miranda declined Mrs. Wainwright's offer

of cookies and milk, preferring to get the lesson over with so she could go straight home. She felt too grim to chat with Mrs. Wainwright as they usually did before each lesson and busied herself instead with fitting her flute together and adjusting the sheets of music on her stand. But she had to smile when she saw Dan's ugly pink pig displayed smack in the middle of the collection on the piano.

She played poorly, her notes faltering, her runs stumbling. After the lesson, Mrs. Wainwright looked at her appraisingly. "There's no sense in my telling you how bad that was. You know exactly how bad it was. Vivaldi would be rolling in his grave. I'm hoping you'll be my star pupil in the spring concert, you know. And April will be here before we're ready if you don't buckle down."

Miranda nodded. "I'm sorry. I guess I just wasn't concentrating."

Surprisingly, Mrs. Wainwright grinned. "I know you've been busy with the Prindle House fund-raisers. And you know I appreciate that—the whole Historical Society appreciates it. But there already are enough people concerning themselves with the old Witch House." She frowned. "In fact, we've just had to change the locks on the doors. Seems some prowlers are around. Of course, the house is mostly empty now, but once we finish setting up the new exhibit, there will be antiques and old documents to protect." She sighed. "Now, Mandy, you've got to keep your mind on your music. And I don't suppose Dan helps one bit, does he?"

"Excuse me?" Miranda looked at Mrs. Wainwright blankly.

She laughed. "Yes, you and Dan do make a lovely couple, dear. But you mustn't let my handsome great-nephew interfere with your music."

For a moment Miranda could only stare at her in confusion, but then she realized Mrs. Wainwright was offering her not one, but two excuses for her poor performance. She had to grin back, grasping at the excuses with relief. "We *have* been working hard. And I like Dan an *awful* lot."

"Ah, young love." Mrs. Wainwright sighed.

Miranda started to pack her flute back into its case. "I should go now," she said. "I'm meeting my mother at her office for a ride home."

"Very well. I'll count on seeing a vast improvement by next week. Agreed? I want you to promise me you'll keep your mind off that handsome boy."

"I promise I'll try." Miranda hurried out into the dark street and began walking back to the town center. She *had* played terribly and she felt badly about that. But she had been thinking, as she had been all day, not of Dan but of Abby. *She's beginning to haunt me*, thought Miranda in annoyance. And she felt like kicking herself for cutting class in order to follow Abby. So what if the girl were a thief? That was a problem for the police, for the school, and for Abby's parents. It was none of Miranda's business.

But how could anyone just disappear like that?

Miranda crossed the common, chilled from the wind and from the uneasy feeling that Abby had been playing cat-and-mouse with her.

When she tramped into her mother's waiting room, Helen was just putting on her coat. "There you are! How was your lesson?"

"Okay." Miranda sank into a chair while Helen said good night to her receptionist.

They walked together to the parking lot. As she unlocked the car door for her daughter, Helen put her hand on Miranda's arm. "Mandy? I'm afraid I've still been worrying about Abby Chandler. Did you get a chance to ask her where she lives?"

Miranda climbed into the front seat and fastened her seatbelt. She stared out the window for a long minute, watching sleet fall through the streetlight. "I asked," she said finally, "but she wouldn't tell me."

CHAPTER THREE

THE NEXT MORNING as Miranda and Dan were walking to their first class, Miranda stopped abruptly outside the principal's office. "Wait a sec, will you?" She peered around the door to make sure Mr. Raphael himself was not there. Puzzled, Dan followed her inside as Miranda, smiling brightly at the secretary, asked for Abby's home address.

"You'll need to ask her yourself, dear," said the woman, looking up briefly from her word processor. "I'm quite busy now."

"But I have a letter I need to send her," lied Miranda. "It's a surprise. If I ask for her address, she'll know something's up."

Now the woman looked interested. "A Valentine's surprise?"

"That's right," Miranda improvised. "She's

new in Garnet and doesn't have any friends yet, really. I thought it would be fun to surprise her."

"Why, isn't that nice, now?" The woman beamed at Miranda. "So many times cards are only exchanged between boys and girls. I think it's real sweet for girlfriends to say how much they like each other." The secretary opened a file and flipped through some computer print-outs. Miranda held her breath as the secretary wrote down an address on a scrap of paper. "Here you go, honey. And you have a nice Valentine's Day yourself now."

"Thank you. You, too." Miranda hurried out of the office with Dan behind her, the paper clutched in her hand. She glanced down at it with satisfaction. *16 Grove Street.*

"What was that all about?" Dan frowned at her.

"I needed her address. My mom still wants to check with her family that she's okay."

"I've never heard you lie before, Mandy. I hope you really are going to send a Valentine's Day card."

Probably I should, thought Miranda. She felt vaguely ashamed of lying. But her interest in the girl was so strong now, she knew that even if her mother didn't want to check out where Abby lived, Miranda would go on her own.

"All right, this shouldn't take long," said Helen that evening after dinner. "At least the snow has stopped. Maybe we'll even get a thaw."

She and Miranda climbed into the car and headed down the hill. Miranda held Abby's address in her gloved hand. "I think Grove Street is over near Mrs. Wainwright's."

The streets were quiet. The street lamps made circles of soft light in the drifts at the sides of the plowed roads. The lights from the houses they passed shone out warmly into the night. Only the old Prindle House was dark. They passed the vacant lot and turned onto Grove, and soon pulled up before a compact white bungalow.

"Sixteen Grove Street," said Miranda. "This is it."

"This shouldn't take long," said Helen, as she got out of the car and stepped over the snowbanks left at the curb by the plows.

They knocked on the front door and waited. The porch light went on and the door opened. "What can I do for you?" A burly man in a bright yellow sweater smiled at them.

Helen introduced herself and Miranda.

"We've come about your daughter. Just to be sure she's all right after her fall."

The man looked puzzled. "How could you know that my daughter fell down?"

Helen explained hastily about the near-miss with the car. "I can't tell you how worried I've been about Abby."

But the man was shaking his head. "Whoa, let's slow down on this one." He held the door open for them to step into the small hallway. Miranda could smell pizza through the closed door to the left of the staircase. "My daughter didn't fall in front of any car. She's eleven months old and just starting to walk, and yesterday she toppled over and bumped her cheek on the coffee table. She's got a little cut, but that's it." He paused. "And her name is Maggie, not Abby. I'm Jim. Jim O'Shaughnessy."

"But isn't this Sixteen Grove Street?" asked Miranda. This wasn't making sense. She knew it was number sixteen. The number had been painted on the porch by the mailbox.

As the man nodded, the door by the stairs opened to reveal a young woman carrying a red-haired baby girl. The baby had a bandage on her cheekbone and was clutching a thick pizza crust in one chubby fist. "Jim? What is it?" asked the woman.

The baby waved the crust at Miranda and gurgled.

Helen explained they had made a mistake. "We must have been given the wrong address, that's all."

"It's the address the school gave me," said Miranda. "Maybe Abby lives next door."

"Well, we know everybody on the street," said the woman, shifting the baby to her other hip. "And I've never met a girl named Abby. Is she your age?"

"I guess so. But she's thin, with long blond hair."

"Sorry." The woman shook her head. "I'm sure I'd know her if she lived around here. We're always looking for baby-sitters."

Miranda and her mother looked at each other. Then Helen thanked the couple and apologized for interrupting their dinner. They said good-bye, and Miranda and Helen trudged back to their car in silence. Once inside, Helen turned to Miranda. "Well, I'm going to call the school tomorrow. I hate to seem to be meddling, but this worries me."

Miranda felt torn between wanting to shrug off the whole mystery of Abby and wanting to know, *needing* to know.

"Probably the secretary just gave you the

wrong address," mused Helen, turning the key.

"Or else Abby gave her the wrong address in the first place."

"Oh, really, Mandy!" Helen glanced at her sharply. "Why would she do that?"

Miranda shrugged, remembering again the disappearing footprints in the snow.

At lunchtime the following day, Miranda and Susannah stood in line at the back of the cafeteria, trying to decide between caramel and strawberry toppings. The menu every Friday featured "Make-Your-Own Sundaes." Even the students who brought their lunches from home delighted in *this* sort of institutionalized food. Dan joined them and pressed his tray gently into Miranda's back.

"Hey, can you come over for dinner tonight?" His voice was low in her ear.

"Well, what are you guys having?"

"What way is that to respond to a dinner invitation?" Dan cried indignantly. "I'm doing the cooking. And you know what that means, don't you?"

"Hamburgers and potato chips."

"O ye of little faith! I've been practicing my culinary arts, I'll have you know. It's going to be a real feast. Say that you'll come."

"I'll come." She grinned at him, glad the look of censure that had been in his eyes since yesterday when she'd lied to the principal's secretary was gone. "Well, I'll have to ask, but I'm sure it'll be fine with my parents."

Dan beamed back at her and she moved on, selecting the caramel topping to go on top of her vanilla and strawberry ice cream, and then spooning on chopped nuts and chocolate chips. A long-faced cafeteria worker squirted a gob of whipped cream onto Miranda's creation. A fleck of cream flew up onto Miranda's cheek.

"Oh, well," joked Miranda over her shoulder to Dan, wiping the cream off. "I *try* to ignore all the signs that we're not in a three-star restaurant, but sometimes it's hard."

"More like negative three," he rejoined. "But wait till tonight. It'll be five stars for me!"

Ahead of them in line, Miranda caught a flash of pale hair. She craned her neck. "Look, Dan—there's Abby."

"So? Don't start, Mandy."

Abby stood in line to pay. Unlike the trays of all the other students, hers held only a single carton of milk. Miranda watched as Abby glanced around furtively and then quickly elbowed the girl in front of her. The girl nearly dropped her tray and she spilled her cup of juice into her sundae.

"Hey!" cried the girl, whirling around. She mopped at her sodden blouse with a paper napkin. "Look what you've done!"

"Don't worry, honey." The woman with the whipped cream can hurried to the rescue with a towel. "We'll have you cleaned up in no time at all. Your boyfriend will never notice the spots."

"Can I have a new sundae? And another juice?" whined the girl. "It wasn't *my* fault it got spilled."

"Don't you worry. Just hold still a minute."

This scene was causing some commotion in the line as people gathered around the disgruntled, wet girl. But Miranda kept her eyes on Abby, who calmly grabbed several cellophane-wrapped sandwiches and a bag of corn chips off the counter and dropped them swiftly into her beaded bag. "Excuse me, excuse me," Abby said, stepping around the cleanup crew on her way to the cash register. "Here, this is for the milk." She handed the cashier some change.

"Thanks," murmured the cashier absently, hunched over a magazine.

"Did you see that?" Miranda whispered.

"I sure did." Dan's voice was grim.

"She just slid the stuff into her bag, cool as anything." Susannah sounded impressed.

"She's a thief. I knew it already, but now we have proof."

"Ssh, Mandy. Not so loud. Let's get our stuff and go talk to her."

They moved ahead to the cashier. "I can't believe anyone would want to steal junk from this place," said Susannah.

But when they had paid for their sundaes and scouted around the large room, there was no sign of Abby at all.

"She's pretty quick with the disappearing act." Miranda led the way to an empty table.

"Well, it's really none of our business, I guess," said Susannah.

"Yeah," agreed Dan. "But she'll get in big trouble one of these days if she doesn't stop it."

Miranda poked unhappily at her ice cream. Why did she have the feeling that Abby was already in big trouble?

At home after school, Miranda sank onto her bed. Friday at last. The week had seemed like forever. A week ago she had never even heard of Abby Chandler. And yet now the girl was like a blister on Miranda's heel, an irritation impossible to ignore.

Miranda tried to do her biology homework, but she couldn't concentrate. So she fished a thick library book out of her backpack and settled herself in the window seat to read until her parents came home. Helen worked until nearly seven every Friday, going over to the hospital at the end of her normal office hours to visit patients and check lab results. Because of the continuing snowfall, she had left her car in the garage today and taken the bus into town. Philip was in Lexington and would pick Helen up at the hospital on his way home.

Miranda liked the silence and peace of the big house. She watched the patterns of late-afternoon light filter across the pages of her book, remembering all too well how elusive that sense of peace had been when her family lived in their cramped New York apartment. There she had tripped over piles of books and papers in the tiny living room to get back to the even tinier alcove that had been her bedroom. Even there it had been hard to have any real privacy, since the walls were so thin she could hear her parents' conversations almost as well as if she were sitting on the couch with them. But here in her big corner bedroom, she had space for all her things, privacy for all her thoughts. And the sounds of the house were muffled. Miranda stretched on the window seat, watching the snow falling outside her window.

Snowing again! She had never known such a white winter before.

Deep in her book, Miranda did not immediately register the thud of the closing front door. But then she marked her page, shut the book, and hurried down the stairs to greet her mother and father and ask about going to Dan's for dinner. "Dad!" She hugged him there in the front hall and unwound his scarf. "You look like a snowman. Where's Mither?"

Then she noticed his grim face and angry frown. "In the kitchen," he said briefly and steered her in that direction.

Puzzled, Miranda pushed through the swinging door, then stopped so fast that her father could not enter from the other side. "Abby!"

Abby stood next to the kitchen table. Her face was as colorless as the winter sky. Her mouth looked pinched, her eyes were wide and staring.

She looks frightened, thought Miranda in surprise. *More than that—she looks terrified.*

Helen was by the sink, shrugging off her coat. When she spoke, her voice was as icy as the weather outside. "I suggest you take off your coat, too, Abby. We need to talk before you can go home."

Abby set her beaded bag on the floor. Then she slowly removed her dirty beige coat and stood holding it. Philip went out the back door and returned in a moment carrying two heavy bags of groceries. "There's another one on the step," he told Miranda, and she opened the back door and hurried to help.

"Okay," said Philip when Miranda set the bag on the table. "Now we talk."

Miranda raised her brows, mystified. What in the world was going on here? She pulled out a chair and sat down at the table.

Abby stood silently, head bowed, as Philip took her coat from her arms and put it on the counter. Helen began unpacking the food from the bags, stowing vegetables in the refrigerator with short, angry movements.

Philip drummed on the table with his fingers. "Can't the groceries wait, Helen?"

Helen shrugged but came over to the table. She sat down and indicated a chair for Abby. Abby sat down slowly and slumped over the table, looking whiter and thinner than Miranda thought possible. For a long moment no one said anything. Both Helen and Philip seemed to be waiting for Abby to speak. But the girl just sat staring at her hands in her lap.

"Would anyone like hot chocolate or some-thing?" asked Miranda to break the silence.

She was stalling, but she was suddenly afraid to hear what was wrong.

"Okay," said her father, surprising her with his unusually gruff tone. "Make us all some."

Miranda left the table and busied herself heating water in the microwave and spooning the cocoa mix into mugs. Philip cleared his throat. "Okay, young lady. Out with it. Why were you breaking into our car?"

Miranda wheeled around to stare at Abby. "You're kidding!"

"She was trying hard, too," Helen told Miranda. "First with a coat hanger, poking around trying to get it in the window crack. We were in the grocery store parking lot. Dad picked me up at the hospital after work, and we did the shopping. We put the bags in the car, then went into the drugstore. When we came out, we saw Abby and rushed over to the car." Helen glanced at Abby's set face and frowned. "Before we could get there, she had taken a brick from her bag and started bashing at the window!"

"You're kidding," repeated Miranda, but she knew her mother was not.

"I figure she was trying to get in to take the

tape player," said Helen, "unless she was going to try to hot-wire the car."

"But—why?" asked Miranda.

"That's what we asked her," said Philip. He put his hand on Abby's bony shoulder, and she flinched as if he had struck her. "She tried to run off, but we caught her."

"Normally we would have taken you— taken any thief—straight to the police," Helen told Abby sternly. "But since I recognized you, and since I've been worrying about you since the day you fell in the road—well, I thought you should have a chance to explain."

Abby suddenly burst into tears. "I said I was sorry! Why can't you just leave me alone?"

"Attempted robbery is too serious to be left alone," said Philip firmly.

"Why in the world would you try to steal our car?" asked Miranda. "Abby, you're too young to drive, anyway."

"I didn't know it was your car, Miranda Browne, or believe me, I would have stayed miles away." Abby's voice was sharp despite her tears.

"You could have recognized it from the day we nearly hit you—," began Miranda, but then remembered that her mother's car was out in the garage. Today they had been driving Philip's car.

"Well, I didn't! It was just there, just like all the other cars in the lot, but it had—," she stopped.

"What did it have, Abby?" asked Philip intently. "Tell me."

Abby ground both fists into her eyes and did not answer.

"Answer him, young lady." Helen's voice was tight.

Abby's voice was barely audible. "All right, all right. It was the food. I saw the bags."

"You mean you were hungry?" questioned Helen.

Abby did not answer.

"I felt we really should call the police right away," Philip told Miranda. "But she begged us not to. Then I said we would call her parents—but she said she doesn't have any. And since I knew she was not just any old thief, but someone who had recently become a household word around here, I said she could come home with us and talk this whole thing out first. I didn't think," he added in a gentler tone, "that she looked like a violent criminal needing to be locked up."

"More like someone needing a good meal?"

Miranda remembered the bulging beaded bag, the bread and peanut butter from the little shop, the sandwiches and chips from the cafeteria.

"And needing someone to talk to," added Helen. "Will you stay for dinner, Abby?"

As Abby's eyes filled with tears, she lowered her head so her hair hid her face like a silk curtain. Then she nodded. "Oh, yes, please."

CHAPTER FOUR

MIRANDA LED a silent Abby upstairs while Philip and Helen fixed dinner. "In here," said Miranda, ushering Abby into her bedroom. The two girls perched in opposite corners of the brightly cushioned window seat. Miranda couldn't think of anything to say to this unexpected visitor.

The silence settled uncomfortably over them as Abby looked around the room. Her glance took in the old-fashioned double bed with its carved wooden headboard and thick quilt, the matching desk and chair, strewn with clothes Miranda hadn't put away, her bookcase well-stocked with old favorites, the dresser, and Miranda's music stand in the corner.

"I play the flute," said Miranda just to break the silence. "Do you play anything?"

Abby took a long time to answer. "Not much . . . these days." Her voice was still choked with tears. "But I used to play the harpsichord. A long time ago. And the piano."

"Well, we have a piano," Miranda began, then stopped as Abby slid down from the window seat and crossed the room to the antique dollhouse in one corner.

"This is beautiful!"

"It's a replica of our house. It was left here by some people who owned the house before we did," explained Miranda politely. "I found it up in the attic when we moved here."

Abby crouched on the floor and looked into the house, taking in the detail of miniature brick, hand-turned porch railings, and tiny drainpipes. "It's perfect."

Miranda decided to be blunt. "Listen, why have you been stealing food, Abby? I saw you steal from the store the other day and from the cafeteria, too."

"It's such a lovely house," whispered Abby.

Miranda crossed the room to her. She saw there were tears on Abby's colorless lashes. "Why the food, Abby?" Miranda persisted. "Why?"

Abby's long, pale hair swung forward to

shield her face like a curtain as she bent over the house. "Look at the tiny brass knocker," she murmured, barely audible. "I've never seen anything like it. . . ."

Miranda gave up and left the room. She went into her parents' bedroom and slouched on the bed, relieved to be away from Abby. She picked up the phone and poked the buttons disconsolately. When Dan answered, she explained that their plans for dinner together must be abandoned. "I can still come over later, I think," she told him. "I'm really sorry. But I have to stay here now and find out what's going on with this weirdo."

"Well," he said, sounding disappointed, "I'll save you some dessert if you promise to tell me all the gory details."

"You've got a deal."

"But Mandy?" He hesitated. "You'll come alone, won't you? I mean, you're not going to bring Abby, right?"

"Do you think I'm crazy?"

"There's enough lasagna here for an army," observed Philip when they were all sitting at the round kitchen table.

Helen served the girls large portions and slipped her husband a small slice. "It's nonfat cheese," she assured him.

He forked some salad onto his plate and passed the bowl to Abby. She piled her plate high. Then, keeping her eyes on her plate, she shoveled the beef, pasta, and cheese into her mouth. She ate hurriedly as if to get her fill before one of them snatched her plate away.

"Slow down," Helen told her gently. "There's lots of food. You can have seconds."

A faint blush colored Abby's cheeks. "Sorry," she muttered.

Helen asked Philip about his work at the museum, and he asked her about her work at the hospital. Miranda realized they must have made a decision not to talk about Abby's assault on their car until later. She joined the conversation, reporting on her classes at school. Only Abby remained silent, chewing steadily.

When all four forks were placed on the plates to signal the end of the meal, Helen pushed back her chair. "There's an apple crumble for dessert—and applesauce for you, Phil. But let's wait a while and digest the lasagna." She raised an eyebrow at Abby. "And talk."

"Really talk," said Philip.

Abby sucked in her breath.

"We're going to need some answers sooner or later, Abby," continued Philip. "Nice, clear answers. We don't want to go to the police about you, and we won't—as long as you'll tell us what's been going on. And we'll have to talk to your family. They need to know about this."

"I think you should know, though," added Helen, "that I called the high school today to see if there had been a mistake with the address they gave us. But the Grove Street number is the one you gave them when you enrolled three weeks ago. Mr. Raphael was very upset to learn it's a false one. Then he contacted the school you told him you went to in Baltimore and discovered it doesn't have accurate records for you, either. It's all very strange." She frowned at Abby. "But does it need to be? What's going on? We only want to help you."

Abby stared at her. When she finally spoke, her voice was tense. "No one can help me."

Helen's frown deepened. "We'd like to try."

"Where do you live, if not on Grove Street?" pressed Miranda. "You have to be living somewhere."

"What right do you have to meddle in my life?" Abby asked shrilly. Her tense, drawn expression and hunched shoulders reminded Miranda of a stray dog she'd once seen in New York, cornered by boisterous boys.

"We have every right to look into the affairs of a thief!" Philip thundered.

"Just leave me alone, all of you." Abby's voice broke with tears. "All week, Mandy has been following me and watching me. I can't bear it anymore."

Philip shook his head. "I don't get it," he said wearily. "Does this really have to be such a mystery? You aren't being fair to accuse us of meddling when you are clearly in some trouble and need the help we would like to give you."

A long moment passed, during which Abby sat with her head down. She seemed exhausted, as if just sitting upright in her chair were an ordeal. Finally she looked up at Helen and Philip and her eyes were tearful. "Well," she said, "I suppose I have to tell you. But there's nothing you can do, though it's nice of you to want to help. It's been so long since I've had anyone to talk to, anyone to trust, I've forgotten what trusting people is like." She took a deep breath, and Miranda could almost see her mind running backward to find a starting point for her story.

They all waited. Outside the kitchen windows it had begun to snow again.

"The truth is that since I arrived in Garnet, I've been living in the old Prindle House. I jimmied the lock on the back door."

At their surprised exclamations, she hesitated, then continued in her soft voice. "I've been on the run for a long time. My parents are dead. They were killed in a fire—years ago. I went to live with my grandfather in Baltimore." Her words came more slowly now, as if chosen with care. "He was an alcoholic and didn't want much to do with me, but he was the only relative I had left. Everyone else is dead. So I sort of took care of him, and he paid for food and stuff. I only went to school sometimes—when I felt like getting out of the house. And when he died, I ran away. I wasn't about to end up in some children's home. So—" This time her pause lengthened into a full minute.

"So? What happened?" asked Helen gently.

Abby shook back her curtain of hair. It cascaded over the back of the oak chair like strands of cornsilk. "So I took money from my grandfather's house, got on a bus, and started traveling. I wasn't sure where I'd end up, but I knew I didn't want to live on the streets. There's too much trouble in that kind of life. I just wanted to be normal, to go to school, to have friends, you know. And when I got off the bus in Boston, I saw an old lady struggling to get onto another bus with some bags of stuff—she had been out shopping, you see. So

I helped her onto the bus, then got on, and rode with her to Garnet. She was so nice, I was—well, I was hoping I could move in with her and kind of help out the way I used to help out my—my grandfather. It's like that with old people, you know. They're often eager to have someone stay and it's so easy. . . ." She broke off and looked around the table at them. "I mean, well, I thought she might need a companion. But I found out she lives in one of those senior citizen communities where you have to be retired. No kids allowed, you know. I liked the look of Garnet, though, so I decided to stay."

Miranda frowned. For a second it had sounded as if Abby meant she'd moved in with old people lots of times. She watched Abby toss back her long hair again and glance more confidently around the table at them. She seemed more relaxed now that she was telling them her story. But Miranda's frown deepened. *Is any of this story true?*

"So you broke into the Prindle House?" pressed Helen.

"Oh, I know it was a terrible thing to do. But I was cold, and the house was empty. At first I meant to stay only a couple of days, until—well, until I could find somewhere else to live. I shopped for food with the money I had left and used my sleeping bag and stuff I'd brought from Baltimore to set up house in the kitchen there. It's the warmest room. After a few days I realized that people were trying to fix up the house and set up a museum or something, and then when I went to school, I learned about the restoration project. I made sure to take all my things out early each morning and hide them in the crawl space under the back porch." She paused and looked at the Brownes as if defying them to comment. "But then a couple days ago people from the Historical Society changed the locks on all the doors. The new locks, they're much stronger and, well. . . ." Her voice trailed off.

"Pick-proof?" suggested Philip drily.

"Well, yes."

"So where have you been sleeping?" Helen asked, her voice gentle.

Abby glanced up from beneath her pale lashes. "Under the porch where I'd hidden my stuff," she said softly. "I thought it would be out of the wind there. But it's awfully cold. I've been hanging out at the library until it closes, then walking around the streets to keep warm until I'm tired enough to sleep. My sleeping bag is pretty good. But then I ran out of money. I had to take food from school."

"And from the corner grocery," said Miranda.

Abby shot her a venomous glance. "Only once. But I never," she hastened to add, looking back at Miranda's parents, "broke into anyone's car before. I hate to steal from people—it seems different with big stores, or the cafeteria. I didn't think anyone would miss the food. I mean, I know it's still wrong, but it's just awful to be hungry and cold. . . ."

Helen looked near tears. She reached over to put her arm around Abby's thin shoulders and hugged her. "The morning we nearly hit you, it seemed you fainted in front of the car. Was that because—?"

Abby nodded, her face clouded. "I hadn't eaten in two days. I tried to sell some of my old things—from my grandfather's house, I mean—at the flea market to get some money. But I sold only one brooch. For three dollars! And it wasn't even really mine to sell, so that was stealing, too. I finally realized I'd have to steal to survive."

Miranda had to admit to herself she was impressed with Abby's resourcefulness. But her father was frowning.

"Abby, there are children's services," he said. "Social workers, lawyers, teachers. Any one of them would be glad to help you."

Abby's expression was bleak. "No. I don't want anything to do with them."

"Listen, of course the things from your grandfather's house were yours to sell. And if you're the only member of your family still alive, as you seem to believe is the case, then surely you'd inherit his house anyway. There might be plenty of money coming to you. You need a lawyer, like it or not."

Abby pressed her lips together and shook her head. After a moment Philip shrugged. "Well, how long were you planning to live like an outlaw?" he asked drily.

She sent him a shy look from beneath her lashes. "I didn't really have a plan," she murmured. "Of course, I knew I couldn't go on for long like this. I suppose I'll move on again when the snow stops. It's always hard to travel in the winters, even when I have some money."

Miranda sat there, puzzling over Abby's story. The girl made it sound as if she had often had to travel in cold winters. There was something about Abby's account that didn't sound right to Miranda. But she couldn't think what it was.

Abby closed her eyes and rested her thin hands atop the tablecloth. "It feels good to tell someone after so long." She opened her eyes then and looked right into Philip's. "I know I was wrong to break into your car for the food, and I know you're going to call the police after all, and I'll end up in a children's home. . . ."

"Oh, no," began Helen.

"Not so fast," said Philip at the same time. They looked at each other. "What are you thinking, Helen?"

Helen checked his face carefully before answering. In his eyes she saw his nod, although physically he didn't move a muscle. Miranda always marveled at the unspoken communication her parents managed so easily. But now she could read the message, too. She braced herself for what was coming.

"Abby," began Helen, taking one of the girl's thin hands in hers, "would you like to stay here with us for a while? Until we can decide what's the best thing to do? I don't think at this point we need to involve the police. I'd rather have you here safe with us. For now. That is, if you want to stay."

"We'll have to talk to the right people, of course," Philip joined in. "A social worker, I guess. And call our lawyer. They'll conduct a search for relatives you may not even know you have. And if you become a ward of the state," he added, his voice warm now, "they would eventually try to place you in a good foster home. Probably you can stay with us while we make inquiries. How would you feel about that?"

Abby nodded eagerly, her eyes shining. "Oh, I'd love to stay with you."

Helen turned to Miranda. "Mandy? What do you think about all this?"

Miranda was fuming. She glared at her parents, but they didn't notice. Both of them had eyes only for Abby, and those eyes were now full of caring and compassion. Miranda drew a ragged breath and expelled it angrily.

"Fine." Her voice was harsh. "I mean, sure, great, we can't very well leave Abby out in all this snow, can we?" She pushed back her chair and stood up. "Look—I'm going over to Dan's now." She carried her plate and cutlery to the sink, then turned back to the table. She saw her parents and Abby sitting there with their empty plates and their big smiles, and she thought they looked like players on a stage. She felt the atmosphere in the big, warm kitchen had changed with Abby inside, as if the snow falling outside had somehow crept in. Miranda longed to escape. "I told Dan I'd come for an hour or so, since I couldn't make it for dinner."

Philip nodded. "Okay, Mandy," he said. "I think Abby looks like she could use a nice, long, hot bath and then an early bedtime."

"We'll make up the fold-out couch in my office," said Helen, already busy with plans. She stood up and began clearing the table. "But first, how about some homemade apple crumble?"

"Oh, yes," said Abby enthusiastically.

"No, thanks," said Miranda. She left the kitchen and ran up to her room. Inside, she stood for a moment, looking around. Was it only food Abby stole, or might she be interested in other things? Miranda saw her favorite silver snowflake earrings on her dresser top and hooked them into her earlobes. Then she snatched up her wallet from the desk. It contained only a few dollars and her library card, but she felt safer keeping it with her. She hesitated. What else to take? On a whim she opened her dresser drawer and fished under her socks for the little stone phoenix. She stuffed it into the back pocket of her jeans.

"Don't be back too late!" Helen called from the kitchen as Miranda bounded down the stairs to the front hall. Abby's voice rang out next, "Bye, Mandy!"

Miranda didn't answer but shivered as she shrugged into her coat. She left her boots by the door and raced outside in her tennis shoes—so great was her hurry to be gone.

CHAPTER FIVE

MIRANDA LAY ACROSS Dan's bed, telling him about it. Her soaking shoes were propped against the radiator. Dan sat across from the bed in an old beanbag chair and rolled the beans beneath the vinyl while she talked.

"Unbelievable," he said at last. "So what's the juvenile delinquent doing now?"

"Probably soaking in the tub. Ripping off all my bubble bath, probably."

Dan shook his head. "That poor thing."

"Hmmm."

"You don't think so?"

"Oh, of course I feel sorry for her. But I don't want her living in my house."

"Come on, Mandy. You're usually so soft-hearted. I mean, I know she's rude and everything. But it sounds like she's had a rough life."

Miranda sighed and flopped over onto her back. "I guess I just don't trust her. She's got this quirky little smile that bugs me to death. I always feel she's mocking me."

"You're paranoid."

Miranda frowned. "Maybe."

"Well, anyway, you missed a first class, five-star meal. The chef was crushed."

"Oh, yeah? What did the chef concoct tonight?"

"House secret. But I'll give you one more chance to try it. Next time."

"You mean you've saved it?"

"Nope. Ate all of it. It was great."

"You ate *all* of it!"

"I'm a growing boy," he said defensively, and she laughed. But it was true, she reflected, looking at him now. He seemed to have grown a full foot in just the past year, shooting up to almost six feet and developing muscles that had the football coach after him to try out for the team. But Dan preferred to spend his time learning about photography or taking long bike rides to neighboring towns. Sometimes Miranda went with him on those rides, and she always marveled at his stamina on the rolling hills.

She stretched on the bed. "It's so peaceful

here. What have you done with Buddy? Did you drug him?" Dan's ten-year-old brother was a great fan of Miranda. She rarely was able to snag time alone with Dan when Buddy was around.

"Better than that. He's away at a friend's house for the night. And my parents are working on the special exhibit at the Prindle House."

"I'm glad Buddy's not here, sweet as he is. I'm really low on energy tonight. Abby just seems to drain me. She gives me a headache, too. I know it's going to be horrible having her at our house."

Dan reached over and switched on his CD player, then slid in a disc. "You need some music to calm you down." He crossed to the bed and sat down beside her. "How about a back rub?"

Miranda felt inexplicably shy. This was simply Dan, her good friend. So why was she studying the cracks on his ceiling to avoid looking at him?

"Go on, turn over," he said. "You're all tense. I give good back rubs."

Then she did look at him. His head was bent low next to hers, and she could see his lashes, short and spiky, framing his dark eyes. "First class, five-star back rubs, I hope."

He grinned. "Absolutely."

She tugged the stone phoenix and her wallet out of her back pockets and set them on his bedside table. Then she turned onto her stomach, and he straddled her thighs, placing his hands on her shoulders.

"Relax," he said. "How can I massage you if you bunch up your shoulders like this?"

"That's your job," she said. "You can't just tell someone to relax. You've got to *make* me relax."

In answer, he pressed his fingers lightly under her shoulder blades, then more firmly. He lifted her hair to prod the nape of her neck. She lay quietly, trying to calm her pulse. All thoughts of Abby and the strange situation awaiting her at home fled from her mind as Dan kneaded her muscles. She tightened up for a moment as she realized he would feel through her sweater that she wasn't wearing a bra. Didn't need one; though she wore one on gym days so the other girls in the locker room wouldn't tease. Then, just when she began to relax, Dan suddenly slid his hands up under her sweater and T-shirt and she tensed again. He rubbed her back in wide, firm circles in time to the beat of the music, his hands warm on her skin. Finally she stopped worrying and just enjoyed the soothing massage.

When the song ended, his hands slowed

then stopped. He let them lie there against her skin for a long moment, palms down, until she made a move to turn and sit up. Then Dan drew his hands out from under her sweater and sat back on the bed.

For a second she could not look at him, but when she glanced over, he was staring at the bedspread, his face flushed. She felt better suddenly, better about being with Dan in this new and exciting way, and even better about Abby's infiltration of her house. "*Well*," she said finally.

"Does your back feel better?"

Miranda, who could not recall having complained her back hurt in the first place, smiled at him. "Much better. Maybe you'd better forget being a museum curator or a photographer and go work at a health club instead."

He laughed and turned up the volume. They sat listening to the music another fifteen minutes or so until Miranda looked at his bedside clock and stood up. "I guess I'd better go. I told my parents I wouldn't be long. Although I doubt they'll miss me when they've got Abby to talk to and fuss over."

"You sound like a jealous only child who doesn't like the new baby."

"Oh, shut up. Abby isn't our new baby.

Don't say such horrible things." She headed for the stairs.

"Hey, don't forget these." He handed her the stone whistle and her wallet from the bedside table and she stuffed them back into her pockets.

Down in the front hall, he loaned her his boots to wear across the drifts back to her house. "My ulterior motive is"—he grinned—"that now you'll have to bring them back early tomorrow."

"How early is early?"

"As soon as I get up. Oh, like after lunch."

Miranda rolled her eyes and darted out the door, carrying her damp shoes. The snow had stopped and the moon peeked through the dark clouds, and Miranda smiled even as the cold wind bit into her. She had the memory of Dan's hands on her back to keep her warm. But as soon as she entered her own house, the smile faded from her face. She could hear gut-wrenching sobs coming from the top of the stairs—from her mother's office. And yet Helen and Philip sat peacefully in the living room, sipping tea and talking before the fire.

"Here's Mandy now," said Philip when she stopped in the doorway, her hands on her hips.

"Can we talk now, sweetheart? Mither and I know you were shocked when we asked Abby to stay, but what else could we have done right then? Sent her back out into the snow? Called the cops?"

Miranda stared at him. "Well, why don't you go to her now, if you care so much? She really sounds awful."

Philip and Helen were on their feet in an instant. "What do you mean?" asked Helen, coming into the front hall.

Miranda kicked off Dan's dripping boots and set them on the mat by the radiator. "What do you mean, what do I mean? Lost your hearing?"

Philip shot her a puzzled glance. "What are you talking about, Mandy?"

From the floor above them, Abby's sobs rose. "Oh, yeah, I guess it's only the wailing of the wind." Miranda couldn't keep the sarcasm out of her voice.

Helen and Philip looked at each other, concern and puzzlement clouding their faces.

Miranda lost her patience. "Come on, you guys! Are you *deaf*? Are you going to let Abby cry like that and not even try to help? I thought you two were the charitable ones around here." She stomped up the stairs. "I don't even want her here. Why do *I* have to play Florence Nightingale?"

At the top of the stairs she threw open the door to her mother's office without knocking. The sofa bed was all made up, its bedclothes rumpled as if Abby had been lying in them. Her sweater and jeans lay in a heap on the desk chair. The beaded satchel sat on the desk. The light was off, but the room was illuminated by soft moonlight. And Abby was not there.

Miranda flung open the closet door, then ran across the hall into the bathroom. Abby was nowhere, yet the crying continued, mournful and deep. Miranda ran to the stairs, frightened.

Her parents were on their way up. "What is it, Mandy?" demanded Philip. "What in the world is going on with you?"

Then the crying abruptly stopped. The house seemed to ring with the sudden silence. Miranda stood there uncertainly. "Are you telling me you didn't hear anything?"

Helen and Philip shook their heads. "We haven't heard a peep out of Abby since she went to bed about a half hour ago," her mother told her. "She was exhausted, poor thing."

"Well, she's not in bed now. Maybe she's out ripping off a few more cars or burglarizing the neighborhood. Maybe we'd better go down and lock up the silverware." What Miranda felt like doing was running downstairs and out the door, back over to Dan's house.

"What do you mean, she's not there?" Philip reached past her and pushed open the door to Abby's room. He flicked on the light switch.

Abby lifted her tousled head from the pillows and stared at them, blinking in the sudden blaze of light. "What—?" she asked in a thick voice, though whether the thickness was from tears or tiredness, Miranda could not say.

Miranda's heart thumped in her chest. *What is going on?*

Helen hurried to her side. "Are you all right, Abby?"

"Oh, yes," she mumbled. "The bed's very comfortable."

"Miranda thought she heard you crying," said Philip from the doorway.

Miranda could see Abby's face in the moonlight as she blinked at them from the bed. Her cheeks were red and her eyes were bright, surely signs that she had been crying. "She did?" asked Abby. "She heard crying?"

"Please come to us if you need anything," Philip said. "Anything at all."

Abby stared at Miranda. "I—I will. But I'm fine. Thank you."

"Sorry to bother you," said Philip, and he ushered Helen and Miranda out into the hall. He closed Abby's door gently. "Now what was that all about, Mandy?"

"She was crying. I heard her," said Miranda flatly. "And then when I looked in the room, her bed was empty."

"Oh, Mandy." Helen shook her head. "Getting us all upset about nothing at all."

"Nothing at all? Mither, I'm telling you, her bed was *empty!*"

"I think we're all tired," said her father. "Let's go to bed now. We can talk more about all of this in the morning." He headed for the master bedroom. "If we must."

Miranda stomped down the hall to her own room. She slammed her door and leaned against it, trembling. From behind her closed door she could hear her parents out in the hall.

"Mandy's just fanciful," Helen said to Philip.

"Well, it's not like her at all. Do you think she's jealous because we're going to try to help the poor girl out for a while?"

Then their door clicked shut, leaving Miranda standing in silence, her fists balled tightly at her sides. *Abby wasn't there—she wasn't, she wasn't.* The words slid through Miranda's mind, wormlike, insidious, and the anger and hurt were replaced by fear. Abby had been crying. She had not been in the room. Then she had reappeared—as if out of thin air.

But that's impossible.

First the vanishing footprints, and now this. The bubble of fear deep inside expanded with each breath Miranda took, and one question pumped in her ears with her heartbeat: *What in the world is going on?*

CHAPTER SIX

IN THE MORNING Miranda blocked the bathroom door while Abby was brushing her teeth. Abby's long hair was tied back from her face with a faded pink ribbon. In the too long, white flannel nightgown, borrowed from Miranda, she looked very small and innocent—almost angelic. But Miranda was not fooled.

"I want to know what's going on." Miranda's voice held all the pent-up hostility and fear of the past night.

"I'm brushing my teeth. That's what's going on. What do you think?" Abby rinsed her mouth and patted her lips with a towel.

Miranda stepped into the room. "I heard you crying. And then you weren't there. So where were you? You'd better tell me, or—"

"Or what?" Abby smirked. "See how I'm

shaking? Trembling with terror of what you might do." She reached back to untie the pink ribbon and shook her hair over her shoulders. Her eyes met Miranda's in the mirror over the sink. "There is no way in the world you could have heard me crying, Miranda Browne. So just put it out of your head. You imagined the whole thing." There was a challenge in Abby's expression, frighteningly at odds with the angelic hair and heart-shaped, pale face.

Miranda stamped out of the room, unsure how to meet that challenge. Abby's laughter followed her down the hall.

Abby settled in quickly, much too quickly as far as Miranda was concerned. Helen moved her files and medical journals to her office in town, and soon the room at the top of the stairs was referred to by all the Brownes as "Abby's room." The sofa bed remained unfolded during the day, and Helen gave Abby a quilt, brightly patterned with blue cornflowers, to cover it. Abby's schoolbooks lay on the desk by the window, and her two dresses and one blouse hung in the closet. She didn't have many personal belongings. Most of what she owned she carried around with her in the bulging beaded bag. Helen promised her a shopping expedition to Boston for some new clothes.

But the hostility between Miranda and Abby grew thicker each day. Abby bristled at everything Miranda said to her, and Miranda counted up all the snide remarks, the insults, and sarcastic comments Abby flung her way, and brooded over them. Miranda spent a lot of time holed up in her bedroom, curled on her window seat, reading or staring out the window at the snow. She could not forget the vanishing footprints and the mysterious crying. She longed for spring. Spring sunshine would melt the snow, and maybe also the icy grip of unease she felt with Abby around.

If only Abby were quieter. That might help Miranda pretend she wasn't really there. But Abby was loud. She had appropriated the old upright piano in the family room at the back of the house and played all the time. Or at least it seemed that way to Miranda, who used to practice her flute in the family room but shunned it now. Abby's music flooded the house.

Helen and Philip were impressed. They urged her to see Mrs. Wainwright about playing in the spring concert. Miranda would be performing on her flute. *Yeah,* thought Miranda. *If I ever get a chance to practice around here.* Abby ducked her head and said she was too shy, but the big house rang with music that seemed anything but shy. Abby played Bach and Mozart and Beethoven with the touch of a master. She played folk songs and ballads, sometimes singing along in a thin, soft soprano. She hammered out boogie-woogie and wrenched out the blues, playing sometimes from memory and sometimes from one of the old, yellowed scores of music she pulled from her beaded satchel. Helen and Philip sang along and sometimes even danced when Abby played. One night Abby taught them the Charleston, and Miranda watched dourly from the doorway as they shimmied, laughing uproariously, across the family room. Another night Abby taught them the steps to a minuet. As the bell-like notes of the simple Bach tune rang out and Helen and Philip faced each other formally to begin, Abby glanced from the music over at Miranda in the doorway. Abby's smile was the quirky, crooked one that made Miranda shiver. She hurried away, back upstairs.

One night after Abby had been with them about ten days, Miranda couldn't keep her anger inside anymore. She had promised her parents she would try to make Abby welcome, but enough was enough. Abby was banging out a fifties' tune, "At the Hop," down on the piano and the house reverberated with the beat. Miranda's head ached. She left her essay for English unfinished and crawled into bed, pulling the quilt over her head. Finally the music stopped. She waited until she heard her parents coming upstairs to go to bed, then left her warm quilt and stalked into their bedroom, plopping herself down into the middle of their big bed.

Philip pulled his sweater over his head and dropped it onto a chair. "Insomnia, Mandy? You have school tomorrow."

"Dad, I can't sleep because I'm going crazy." Tears pressed hotly behind her eyes.

Helen sat down next to Miranda on the bed. "Mandy? You're crying! What is it, honey?"

Miranda shook her head. "No, I'm not crying. I just have a headache. But, Mither— oh, how much longer does she have to stay? It feels like forever already. I can't stand it."

Philip sank onto the bed, too. "I take it 'she' refers to our houseguest across the hall?"

"I mean it. Having her here is making me sick. All her nasty little digs at me. And that *piano!* I'm *trying* to live with her, but all I can think of is that soon she'll have to go. I'm practically crossing the days off on my calendar."

Philip's face creased with a frown. "Hey, I didn't know you felt like this. I thought things were working out."

"I guess I did, too," added Helen.

"You both must be blind, then. And deaf." Miranda scrubbed her hands through her hair. "We can't be in a room for two seconds without fighting. She's always giving me nasty looks and saying obnoxious things—like how immature I am. Me? *She's* the one who had better grow up, if you ask me. Her piano playing is driving me nuts. I know you want me to be a good hostess, and I've been trying not to let her bug me, but I just *can't* anymore. She doesn't seem like a guest at all—it's like she's digging her heels in." *And she can make herself vanish*. That was the worst thing of all.

Helen reached over and smoothed back Miranda's dark curls. "What do you mean, Mandy?"

"I just don't trust her. Don't you feel it, too? She's holding something back—I don't know what. I just feel . . . oh, I don't know. Kind of weird whenever she's around." She wanted to say something about the footprints and crying, but didn't. She couldn't bear hearing them say again that she was just jealous.

Philip said it anyway. "Seems to me you feel threatened by her. But why? Her being here doesn't take anything from you, honey." He lay back and tossed a pillow into the air, catching it lightly, "I mean, think about that. She's in a terrible position."

"I know you just think I'm jealous, but it isn't that." Miranda bit her bottom lip. "She makes me uneasy. She makes me *cold*." She thought for a second. "Threatened—but not in the way you mean, Dad. I'm *not* jealous of Abby. She makes me . . . she makes me feel queasy."

Philip smiled. "Queasy?"

"OK, so it sounds dumb. But she gives me the creeps." Miranda bit back the real reason: *She can disappear!*

"Wow." Helen sighed. "I like Abby a lot." Miranda steeled herself as Helen continued. "Dad and I hoped we might let her stay a bit longer. Until her relatives are found. You know, we feel you've been an only child for too long."

"Then have a baby, Mither!"

"I don't think you know how hard we've tried to," said Philip quietly.

"Funny, isn't it," murmured Helen. "I help infertile couples all the time but haven't managed to do anything for us. Now we don't want a baby anymore, Mandy. But if we can help out by having Abby stay a while. . . ."

"I can't believe this! Now you're talking as

if you're planning to adopt Abby tomorrow." Miranda felt panic rising in her. They just didn't understand.

"No one is talking about adoption." Helen stood up, wandered over to the window, and looked out into the snowy night. Then she turned back. "I know it's a big change having her here, Mandy. But—"

"But what you're saying certainly alters things," Philip interjected. "If you're miserable, of course she'll have to go. Still, I'd like you to try especially hard to settle things with her. Maybe there's some problem you girls can work out together. Maybe talking will help. Do you think?"

Miranda shrugged. "I really don't think you understand anything I've been trying to tell you. It's not just a personality conflict. There's something about her. Something . . ."

"Weird," finished Helen. "So you keep saying."

"Look, will you at least tell her to cut out all the piano playing? I can't practice my flute anymore, or even do my homework, with all her noise."

"All right, Mandy," said Philip. "I'll talk to her about cutting down. But it is a shame to restrict the one thing that seems to make her really happy." Philip gave her a hug. "Now get back to bed. It's nothing to lose sleep over. Agreed?"

"Not really."

He sighed. "Good night, sweetheart."

One Monday after school, Helen picked up Miranda, Abby, and Susannah and drove to the Revere Mall, a huge complex of department stores, specialty shops, and restaurants on the outskirts of Boston. Abby sat up front next to Helen and chattered excitedly, her pale face flushed. She seemed childishly eager, thought Miranda, to shop for the new clothes Helen had promised. Miranda sat in back with Susannah. She had invited her friend along after Helen made it clear there was no getting out of this shopping expedition. Miranda hoped she and Susannah could slip away and browse in a bookstore or something while her mother and Abby bought out the junior department at Macy's.

"You need a new pair of jeans and of course underwear and socks," Helen told Abby. "Also a skirt or two. And what about a new nightgown? Miranda's is really too big for you. A heavy flannel nightgown would keep you cozy in this weather."

"You make it sound like I sleep out in the snow, Helen," objected Abby. "I always feel warm at your house. It's so cozy and . . . and safe."

"I'm glad." Helen took one gloved hand off the steering wheel and reached over to pat Abby's knee.

Miranda crossed her arms across her chest and stared hard out the side window. Her head was aching again. She watched the bare trees blur as their car zipped past.

"What about you, Susannah?" asked Helen. "Are you up for some fashion shopping?"

Susannah leaned forward, laughing, and brandished her mother's credit card. "I'm armed and dangerous!"

Abby giggled softly from the front seat. She seemed unusually animated today, more like a normal teenage girl than before. But Miranda suspected Abby was anything but normal. She dug her elbow into her friend's ribs. She couldn't bear to have Susannah falling in with Abby's high spirits. She needed Susannah to sustain *her*. But her friend was acting like a traitor now, leaning forward to discuss with Abby the best color choices for people who had blond hair, as both of them did. Miranda fingered her own dark curls and frowned out the window until they arrived at the mall and parked.

Inside the department store, she sat outside the dressing room and rubbed her throbbing temples while her mother and Susannah dashed all over the place to find items for Abby to try on. They chose cotton turtlenecks, colorful sweaters, and skirts, handing them to Abby when she peeked around the concealing curtain. Helen wanted to come in to help, but Abby wouldn't let her.

"Oh," she said in wonder, coming out to model the first outfit, "Is it really me? I look like a whole new person. Don't you think? Now I feel like a real modern-day girl!"

"You look like a *fashionable* girl, that's for sure," said Helen. "And very pretty, too. The bright colors make you look less pale. Now, try on the other things. And before we go, I'd like to find you a winter jacket. The beige one you have is really worn quite thin."

Miranda waited quietly while they trooped out to search for a coat. After about ten minutes they came back to the dressing room in triumph, and Abby modeled a thickly quilted denim jacket. "What do you think?" Helen asked Miranda.

"It's fine." Miranda gave Abby a small smile. The pale girl beamed at herself in the mirror. She seemed astonished at her transformation.

Miranda stood up from the little stool and picked up her own coat. "Can we go now?"

"I still want to get Abby some underwear and a nightgown," said Helen. "And a pair or two of shoes. The ones she has now are worn out and unsuitable for the weather."

"You can wear your new things to the Valentine's Dance, Abby," said Susannah as they left the dressing room. "You *are* going to that, aren't you?" Carrying the other clothes, Helen walked over to the saleswoman to pay.

"Oh, no," said Abby. She stopped before a full-length mirror and turned this way and that, admiring her new jacket.

"Why not?" pressed Susannah. "It could be fun. Mandy and I are on the committee to decorate the gym. It's going to be so pretty. You haven't really gotten to know any of the kids, Abby. This would be a good time."

Helen beckoned to Abby. "Come over here, Abby. The salesclerk needs to see the tag on your coat."

As she obediently walked away, Abby spoke over her shoulder to Susannah. "Kids these days don't really know how to dance at all." Her voice was emphatic. "It's so dumb the way they just leap around. School dances are always so embarrassing."

Susannah looked at her in surprise, but Miranda narrowed her eyes. *Kids these days?* As if Abby were so much older. "Ignore her," she hissed to her friend, and then trailed behind as her mother led them to the shoe department, where Abby selected a pair of pink high-tops and some bright yellow, fleece-lined waterproof boots.

"I'm beginning to see what you mean," said Susannah a few days later when she and Miranda were making brownies after school. They had come to the Johnstons' house especially to avoid Abby, who always went straight home after school. "Half the time I think Abby might want to be friends, but as soon as I try to get close to her, she says something totally nasty or weird. I mean, she says hello in the hall, and she loaned me a pen when I left mine in my locker, but whenever I ask if she wants to eat lunch with us or something, it's like she's deliberately nasty." Susannah looked insulted. Miranda was sorry to see her friend's feelings hurt but was also secretly relieved. She couldn't bear it if Susannah fell for Abby as thoroughly as her parents had.

Miranda measured out a cup of chopped walnuts and stirred them into the brownie mix. Susannah poured the batter into the buttered pan and slipped the pan into the oven. They sat at the table to wait. Susannah flicked back her blond ponytail and glanced at the clock. "Eighteen minutes. How can we wait that long?"

Miranda opened her backpack and drew out the school newspaper. "Have you seen Dan's photos of the Prindle House? They turned out really well. I wish we could have stayed longer that day, but you know Abby." She slid the paper across the table. She and Abby had stayed only for the ceremony when the Student Council presented the money raised from the flea market to the Historical Preservation Society. A lot of the other students started work on the house right after the ceremony, following the directions of the carpenters, but Abby, who seemed bored by the whole preservation project, demanded they go home. Abby never let on she had been in the Prindle House before, and Miranda kept her secret.

Susannah studied the photos Dan had taken. There was a shot of Mrs. Wainwright, as Historical Society President, surrounded by high school students and beaming as she held up their check. There was a picture of students setting to work to repair the staircase. Susannah was in the foreground, brandishing a hammer.

"Hey, I'm famous!" She laughed, then jumped up to check on the brownies.

Miranda was always hungry after school, especially on snowy days, and her hunger grew as the smell of warm chocolate filled the kitchen. She was enjoying the peace and warmth of the Johnstons' house—and the silence of no piano music—when the back door opened and Susannah's mother entered, wiping her snowy boots on the mat.

"Hi, girls! Nice to see you, Mandy." She held the door for the frail, elderly woman with a cloud of white hair who came in slowly behind her, leaning with one gnarled hand on an aluminum-frame walker. The other arm was encased in a white cast.

"Nonny!" cried Susannah, leaping up to hug her. "You're back!"

Miranda grinned. She was very fond of Susannah's great-grandmother. The old woman had been born in Garnet, right in the house where Miranda's family now lived. Miranda enjoyed hearing stories about her house in the old days when Nonny was a little girl. Nonny was in her nineties now and growing increasingly frail. After her husband died last winter, Susannah's parents urged her to move in with them, and she did. She had recently been hospitalized with a badly broken arm after a fall on the icy front steps.

Susannah patted Nonny's uninjured arm. "Is your suitcase in the car, Nonny? Shall I bring it in?"

"Thank you, my dear, but your dad's fetching it." Nonny sniffed the air appreciatively. "Smells good in here."

"We were making a batch of brownies for our after-school snack," Susannah told her. "We didn't know you were coming home from the hospital today, or we'd have made them in your honor."

"Well," declared Miranda, "as it is, we'll *eat* them in your honor. There's enough for everyone."

Susannah's mother joined them, and they all sat at the table devouring the rich, fudgy brownies. The adults had cups of tea and the girls had milk, and Miranda felt light and easy and free. It was so nice to be celebrating something, so nice to sit with a family that was not full of tension. How sad, she reflected now, that her own house no longer afforded her peace and serenity. Since Abby had come to stay, everything was different.

"How are your flute lessons coming along?" Nonny asked her great-granddaughter.

"I'm as hopeless as ever." Susannah sighed. "Mandy might make the big time someday, but not me—at least not with a flute." Susannah wanted to be a doctor. "But look at this, Nonny." She opened the school newspaper and pointed to her picture. "If I can't make it into medical school, maybe I'll take up carpentry."

The old woman adjusted her glasses and held the newspaper at arm's length in her good hand. "My goodness, Susie. You look just like a boy in those overalls and that cap! In my day I'd never have been allowed out to a public ceremony dressed like a ragamuffin." But she smiled.

"Look, here's Mandy," said Susannah, tapping the photo of Mrs. Wainwright surrounded by students. "She's wearing overalls, too."

Nonny shook the paper and held it up to see. "Ragamuffins, the pair of you. That's what I say." Then suddenly her smile turned into a look of surprise.

"What is it?" asked Miranda. "Can you see me? I'm right here, in the front."

"Oh, I see you, dear. It's this other girl I'm looking at. There's an astonishing resemblance to a child I had in one of my classes once—oh, years and years ago." At one time or another Nonny had probably taught most of the residents of Garnet until she retired about thirty years earlier. Her gnarled finger poked at the image of the pale girl with blond hair standing right beside Miranda. "Take her out of that sweater and jeans and put her in a dress, and she'd be a dead-ringer. . . ."

The girl standing next to Miranda in the photo was Abby. Miranda felt a leap of fear. Nonny shook her head and put down the paper. "I've seen so many kids in my time, it's hard to remember them, but that was one girl I'll always remember."

"What happened?" asked Susannah. "Was she a troublemaker?"

"It was a sad case. But sometimes you have to get involved, like it or not."

Susannah's mother looked up from her brownie, interested. "Was it something at her home? Did you have to intervene?"

Nonny shook her head. "Not exactly. The problem was, she didn't have a home. And when I found out, I reported her to the authorities, and they took her off to the orphanage." She tapped the paper again. "That was the old Prindle House, you know, in the 1930s. In one of its many incarnations." She sighed. "I thought I was doing the right thing, of course, but apparently the girl hated it there. She ran away and no one ever found her. I often wondered what became of Abby."

Miranda spoke up excitedly. "That's her name, too! I mean, the girl in the picture is named Abby, too. And she doesn't have a home, either. She ran away from Baltimore when her grandfather died, and now she's living with us."

Nonny laughed. "I love coincidences like this. Isn't it amazing?"

Mrs. Johnston frowned. "I wonder if there's any connection. Don't see how there could be, really, but—"

Miranda interrupted her. "Maybe the girl Nonny knew was Abby's mother! No, she'd be too old. Well, her grandmother, then. And maybe that's why Abby came to Garnet when she left Baltimore—to find out more about the other Abby."

"How very strange," said Nonny. "Well, will you ask her—this Abby of yours? I'd like to know what she says." She sighed. "Guess I've always felt a little bit guilty about my

Abby. She must have been unhappy to have run away like that."

"Well, I'll ask Abby tonight if she knows anything about it," Miranda promised.

"Ask *your* Abby, you mean," laughed Susannah.

"Ugh, don't call her that!" Miranda stood up to leave. She put on her coat and boots and shouldered her backpack. Her mittens and house key fell out onto the floor, and there was a flurry of arms reaching out to set her straight. Mrs. Johnston handed back the gloves with a grin. Nonny handed back her key.

"All set now?" asked Mrs. Johnston. "Do you mind walking? Or shall I try to take you?"

"Oh, no, I don't mind walking. In all this snow, it would probably take longer by car."

Miranda hugged them all good-bye, then trudged out to the street. The late afternoon sun was low, and the bitter wind blew right through her. She hurried along the newly plowed sidewalk as fast as she could. Here she had hoped an afternoon at Susannah's house would be a respite from thoughts of Abby. *Was there no escape?* Miranda groaned to herself as she started up the hill to her house. She seemed doomed to be haunted by Abby, one way or another.

CHAPTER
SEVEN

MIRANDA CARRIED the salad to the table and sat down across from Abby. "Well," she began brightly, "Nonny's out of the hospital already."

"That's good," said her father. "I hope the Johnstons will be able to convince her to leave the snow shoveling to them from now on."

"I doubt it. She's a pretty amazing old lady." Miranda paused, waiting for Abby to ask who Nonny was. But the other girl helped herself to the salad without comment.

"We showed her the school newspaper article about the Prindle House project, and she said in her day girls didn't go around wearing overalls."

Miranda's mother smiled. " 'Her day.' That's such a funny expression. Sounds like the only real time of your life is when you're young. And, of course, that isn't true. It's as much old Mrs. Johnston's day now as it ever was."

"Well, she doesn't think so," replied Miranda. "Or maybe she was just talking about how girls look now, and how they looked when she was our age. I don't know. But she thought *one* girl in the paper looked pretty interesting."

She paused and looked pointedly at Abby, who did not respond. After a moment Helen smiled obligingly and asked: "And which girl was that?"

"Abby."

Now Abby raised her head, eyes alert. "What do you mean?"

"I'll show you the picture," Miranda said with satisfaction and reached for her backpack on the counter. She pulled out the newspaper. "See? There you are, right next to me. Nonny saw you and said you looked exactly like a girl she taught years and years ago. Well, exactly like you, except for the clothes. It was in the 1930s, I think Nonny said. The other girl's name was Abby, too."

Although Abby's face remained blank, Helen and Philip looked interested, so Miranda continued. She told them the story of how Nonny had alerted the authorities that the other Abby was homeless, how the girl had been sent to live in the Prindle House orphanage, and how she had run away. "No one ever saw her again. So we wondered whether you knew anything about her."

"That's fascinating," said Philip. "But it's probably a coincidence."

"Or is there something to it?" asked Helen. "Abby, is that why you came to Garnet—were you tracing your roots?"

Abby shook her head.

"She might have been your grandmother, Abby," Miranda said.

"She wasn't."

"Or some other family connection."

"My grandparents were from Baltimore. I never heard any story about one of them being in a children's home." Her voice was louder than usual.

"Well, I'll take you over to meet Nonny sometime," said Miranda. "Even if there's no connection, she'll get a kick out of seeing you since you look so much like the girl she knew all those years ago."

"I don't want to meet her," said Abby.

"Oh, why not try to make somebody happy for once?"

Abby's frown was as sharp as her voice. "It's nothing to do with me."

At a reproving glance from her mother,

Miranda bit back a sharp retort. She carefully rolled up a forkful of spaghetti. She chatted with her parents, ignoring Abby across the table as completely as if she weren't there at all.

After dinner the four of them gathered in the big living room. Miranda lay sprawled in front of the fireplace, a bowl of popcorn within easy reach. Abby curled up in an armchair, one shoulder turned away from the fire, away from Miranda. Both girls were reading *As You Like It* for their English classes. Helen and Philip stretched out in their customary places on either end of the long couch, feet touching. They all read in silence until a pine bough exploded with a dramatic pop and burst of sizzling blue flame, and Abby yelped.

"Oooh!" It was a small cry, but full of real fear. She clapped one hand over her mouth.

"Abby? What is it?" Helen put her book on the coffee table and stood up.

But Abby shook her head, fear still bright in her eyes. "Nothing, nothing really. I just don't like fire very much. After what happened to my parents. . . ."

"How about if I make us some cocoa?" asked Philip, offering his usual remedy for just about anything. "It's the perfect thing for a cold, snowy night. *And,*" he added gravely, "no fat and no sugar."

"Let's just hope they left the chocolate in," said Miranda as her father left the room.

"Look at that snow." Helen pointed to the window. "I've never seen weather like this."

"I'm sick of it," grumbled Miranda. "It's lasting forever."

"Don't get too sick of it. This is only February," Helen reminded her. "We'll have snow until April, at least. You'll really be suffering a long time if you come down with spring fever now."

"This isn't really so bad," Abby spoke up. "I've seen worse. Real blizzards, and people stuck in the mountains, and well—much worse than this."

"Where?" grumbled Miranda. "The mountains of Baltimore?"

Abby didn't answer, and Miranda flopped onto her stomach and buried her face in the carpet. "Ugh. February is totally dreary. Nothing to do, nothing to look forward to—"

Helen laughed. "Poor thing. Don't forget the dance."

"Oh, right—the Valentine's Dance." She felt slightly more cheerful.

A call came from the kitchen for Helen to come locate the hot chocolate mix. "I can only find the old mix," Philip complained loudly. "The poison. Where's the stuff I bought?"

Helen rolled her eyes at the girls and went to help him.

When they were alone, Abby snorted. "So you'll be going to the dance with the other silly children, jumping around, stomping on everybody's toes. Nobody knows how to dance anymore."

Miranda tried to snort just as unpleasantly. "Speak for yourself. I can dance."

Abby raised one corner of her mouth in the smirky grin Miranda hated. "I doubt that, Miranda Browne. You have no idea what dancing is. Real dancing. The minuet—or the waltz—"

"Give me a break," Miranda snapped. "At least the dance is for a good cause." Who was Abby to act so superior? A runaway from the streets of Baltimore! Was that where she learned to waltz?

Miranda turned back to her book resolutely. When her parents came back with hot chocolate, she sipped her drink and continued reading, uninterrupted except by the crackling of the new wood Philip put onto the fire and by the murmurs of conversation he and Helen exchanged from their ends of the couch. When she finished the play, Miranda sat up and stretched. Time to head up to bed. But just then Helen closed her book, too.

"I think we should talk about it tonight, Phil."

"Right. Time to see what the girls think."

Abby, who had been dozing in the big armchair, her book face down on her lap, raised her head. Miranda tensed, bracing herself for whatever was to come. She could tell by the pleading look her mother gave her that she wasn't going to like it.

Helen rubbed her hands through her feathery dark hair and glanced at her husband for support. Philip leaned forward on the couch and cleared his throat. Still no one spoke. For a second Miranda imagined them all held in a giant's palm, waiting for the fist to clench.

"We've had a few weeks together now," Helen began, smiling at Abby, "and we feel good about having you with us. I know you and Mandy have some problems to work out, but I'm sure you'll manage. Phil and I have been wondering what your plans are now. Where you want to go next—what you hope to do. Because—"

Philip spoke up as she hesitated. "Because we've spoken to a social worker, and she said since there's been no progress tracing any family members, you could stay with us through March."

"Whether you stay with us or not depends

on a lot of things," said Helen. "A lot of them are legal details to work out, but most important for us is whether you and Mandy feel comfortable with our arrangement. We would want you to look on this as your home and on us as your family while you're here."

Miranda saw the grateful tears spring to Abby's eyes. But before Abby could speak, Miranda opened her mouth and surprised even herself with the vehemence of her anger. *"No way!"*

Then, seeing the hurt on Abby's face and the surprise on her parents' faces, she tried to temper her words. "It's—it's just hard. I mean, I know you should live here rather than go back out on the streets. I wouldn't want to send you to an orphanage, or anything, like that girl Nonny knew all those years ago. . . ." She didn't look at any of them, but stared at the fire, lips pressed tightly together. She must not let them see her fear.

"Mandy, honey." Philip was at her side, kneeling on the floor. "We're talking about one more month. Just through March, that's all we're saying. We'd just be Abby's foster family while the authorities keep trying to locate her relatives. Another few weeks won't seem very long at all. It won't be so hard."

Miranda clenched her teeth. What did he know about it, anyway? "It's harder than you think."

"Evidently." Helen spoke drily. She began gathering the mugs onto the tray.

"But our offer still stands, Abby," added Philip, his face unreadable. "If you girls work things out, let us know. We'd like you to stay through March. After that—we'll have to see."

Then Abby's voice, icy and tight, slapped his words away. "Thank you. I'd like to stay, but how can I?" She whirled on Miranda. "What makes you think it isn't hard for me, too, Miranda Browne? You're no bargain either, let me tell you. I've never met a girl who takes as much for granted as you do. You think you deserve all the good fortune you have? What a laugh! You make me sick!"

Then she turned to Miranda's parents, who were regarding both girls with closed faces. "I'm very sorry. You've both been perfectly wonderful to me. But you must see that I couldn't stay with—" Her voice broke, and she jumped out of her chair and ran from the room. They heard her footsteps pounding up the stairs. This time they *all* heard her sobs.

Helen looked helplessly from Miranda to Philip. Then she left them and ran upstairs after

Abby. Miranda's stomach was so knotted, she wondered for a moment whether she would actually be sick. Philip handed her the tray of empty mugs.

"Let's wash this stuff" was all he said.

She followed him into the kitchen. "*You* see how awful things will be if she stays here, don't you, Dad?"

He didn't answer but turned the water on full force to fill the sink.

CHAPTER EIGHT

MIRANDA DRESSED CAREFULLY on Saturday evening. She tried on a swirly peasant skirt that had been a birthday gift from her aunt Belle and studied herself in the mirror on the back of her door. She wasn't sure which type of blouse would look best with the multi-colored skirt. She held up two: a light blue silk T-shirt from India and a lacy white cotton blouse her mother had bought her to wear to a cousin's wedding last summer. She draped first one and then the other across her chest and twirled in front of the long mirror. Then, feeling foolish, she tossed them both on the bed.

What did she think this was—a summer garden party? It was freezing out, and the party was only a dinner at Dan's. He had been rather formal, though, when he asked her on Thursday to reserve Saturday night for him.

"I'm cooking," he had said, then added, "wear something appropriate."

"Like a bib, you mean?" she teased. "To catch all the hamburger grease and ketchup?"

"Don't you have an evening gown or something?"

"Listen, I'll wash my jeans in your honor."

She had decided only minutes ago to attempt a festive look. After all, usually Mrs. Hooton cooked for the family. This was a special effort Dan was making, and she wanted to show she appreciated it. After dinner they'd probably go up to his room to listen to music the way they usually did. *Maybe he'll give me another back rub.*

She heard a tinkle of keys, and Abby's piano music flooded the house with ragtime. The bouncy, toe-tapping beat made Miranda's head ache. She turned from the mirror, grabbed her usual baggy green sweater out of the bottom drawer of her dresser, and pulled it on. This would have to do. She threaded silver earrings in her ears, left the dressy blouses crumpled on the bed, and hurried downstairs.

Her parents were shimmying around the kitchen while they prepared dinner together. They waved from the doorway as Miranda shrugged into her heavy coat and boots. *What goofs.* She left the house, pulling the heavy front door closed on the rollicking piano music. She trudged across the street, snow crunching underfoot. Her headache receded as Dan opened the door even before she pressed the bell. Light from the house shone out in warm welcome around him.

He looks different, thought Miranda, studying him. Although he wore his usual jeans, his shirt was one she had never seen before, and he had borrowed one of his father's corduroy jackets. Dan's dark hair was carefully combed, and he smelled faintly of some unidentifiable aftershave. Miranda wondered whether he really did shave and, if so, why he had never told her about it before. It was the sort of news they would have shared—before. *Before things started changing between us,* she thought. She smiled at him, suddenly regretting the baggy green sweater after all.

"Right on time," he said, and ushered her into the front hall.

"You said seven on the dot, and so here I am." She unzipped her coat, looking around for the other Hootons. Usually Buddy was the first to bound into the hall to greet her. But only Dan was there. "Where's Buddy? Where are your parents?"

"We have the house to ourselves." He actually helped her take off her coat. She looked at him incredulously. Should she offer him the chance to remove her boots as well? But he made no move toward her feet, so she slipped the boots off herself, and started through the dining room to the big, cozy kitchen.

"No, wait," he said, catching her elbow. "In here."

Surprised, she followed him into the living room. The cavernous living room was not often used at the Hootons' in winter because it was too large to be heated properly in cold weather. The big double doors into the front hall were normally kept closed, the draperies pulled across the long windows, and the upholstered furniture covered with old sheets to keep off the dust. In warmer months the room was a gathering place for the whole family, but winter found them back in the old-fashioned kitchen, seated around the old oak table or curled up on the battered couch.

Miranda raised her brows now as she took in the changes in the living room. Two-thirds of the room remained in shadow, the furniture still covered with sheets. But the far section of the room beckoned warmly. Dan had pulled a table close to the roaring fire in the large brick fireplace and set it with a linen cloth and what Miranda thought she recognized as Mrs. Hooton's best antique china. Long tapered candles in silver holders stood sentry on the table next to a bouquet of dried flowers. Dan had pulled a love seat close to the fireplace and piled pillows and an afghan on the floor. Soft light beckoned Miranda onward across the room till she stood before the fire.

"This is—nice," she said to Dan, who was looking at her expectantly. "But a little strange. I mean—why in here? Why not in the kitchen—as usual?"

"I don't want things to be usual," answered Dan. "My parents and Buddy are in Cambridge until tomorrow night. I wanted some time with you. Without parents and little brothers. Or Abby. You know, *alone*."

Miranda smiled slowly at him, but felt cut off from the rest of the world here in this big, shadowy room, with the rest of the house stretching endlessly around them. Her own parents and Abby in their kitchen across the street seemed miles away.

"What's wrong?" asked Dan. "Don't you like a little atmosphere to set the mood?"

"The mood for what?"

"For dinner, of course," said Dan. "Do you want some wine?"

Miranda shook her head, gazing at him steadily. "No thanks."

"Come on, not even a drop?" He walked over to the table and poured a glass of red wine. "It's called retsina, and it's supposed to go with the meal." Dan swirled the wine in the glass, then held it up to the fire. "Look at that. Isn't it beautiful?"

"It is, but I'll just have water." Miranda could hear the wind rise outside the heavily curtained windows, could sense the whirl of white as the snow blew up from the drifts.

"Water's not right on a night like this. I'll warm up some apple cider." Dan left the wine glass on the table and crossed the room to switch on some music. The strains of a Vivaldi concerto filled the room. *The Four Seasons*," Dan said. "To bring a little bit of spring into winter."

"My favorite music," murmured Miranda.

"I know," said Dan with satisfaction. "Now, dinner is just about ready, so you wait here and I'll heat up the cider and bring everything in."

"Can't I help?"

"No, you just hang out here by the fire and stay warm. I'll only be a minute."

He left the room and Miranda sank onto the pillows in front of the fireplace. She listened to the music and thought how long it had been since she'd played her flute. Mrs. Wainwright was getting impatient.

Miranda watched the flames and waited for Dan. The candles on the table flickered. In the dim light the mounds of covered furniture were distant hills. The table and love seat, gilded by firelight, formed a shelter. The Vivaldi soothed her. It erased Abby's thumping piano from her head.

In a few minutes Dan returned with a tray of steaming food. He set it on the table with a flourish. She blinked, turning from the fire as if coming out of a trance, and stood to help him serve the meal.

He had worked hard, she saw that immediately. One large bowl held fluffy rice, another a green salad with tomatoes and wrinkled olives. Small bowls held crumbled feta cheese and nuts. There was a casserole of layered lamb, eggplant, and mushrooms in a thick sauce of cheese and garlic and basil. The aroma made Miranda's mouth water.

"This is called moussaka," Dan said, scooping up a slice of the casserole and putting it on her plate. "It's Greek."

"Well, I'm impressed," she admitted.

"I was going to try to make something called dolmas," he told her, "which are grape leaves wrapped around a filling—but this seemed a better bet."

"How did you learn to cook like this? Are you sure your mom isn't hiding out in the kitchen? The last food you cooked me was—" She broke off, and he grinned.

"You mean the hamburger mixed with tuna? That was when I was a mere child."

"Yeah—last August!"

Their laughter relaxed them and dispelled the formal feeling. They sat down to eat, chatting as comfortably as always. Dan inquired about things at home, how Abby was doing, but Miranda shook her head. "Don't ask. I just want one night of peace when I don't have to look at Abby or hear Abby or talk about Abby! I don't even want to *think* about Abby."

Dan held out his hands as if to fend her off. "Okay, okay, the name won't pass my lips again tonight."

Miranda looked at him slyly over the flickering candles. "What name?"

They talked about the Prindle House project, about school, about the upcoming dance. "Let's go to the dance with Susannah and the kids from the school newspaper," suggested Miranda. "Unless Susannah goes alone with

Dave Dunlop. I know that's what she's hoping."

Dan frowned. "That egomaniac? I don't know what girls see in him. He's such a jerk. I think she should come with us."

But Miranda remembered how eagerly Susannah spoke of going out on real dates soon—alone with a boy. She didn't seem content anymore with their group activities. "In any case, the dance will be fun—even if we can't dance very well."

"Who says we can't dance?"

"Oh—nobody." Miranda cast Abby's mocking smile resolutely out of her mind.

After dinner Dan cleared the table, refusing Miranda's offers of help. She settled herself on the love seat, but when Dan returned with a plate of little cakes, he sat on the floor in front of the fire and patted the space next to him.

She slid to the floor and pushed a pillow against the love seat behind her back. They watched the fire, and Miranda was freshly aware of the empty house all around them. "Well, that was really a great meal," she said to break the silence. "You get an A⁺."

"I'll be sure to tell my mom when she gets home." He held out the plate of cakes. "These are baklava."

"What do you mean, tell your mom?"

Miranda bit into one of the sweet pastries con- cocted of layers of tissue-thin dough, sugar, cinnamon, chopped nuts, and honey. The bite melted in her mouth. "Mmmm," she said. "Are you telling me your mom cooked these after all?"

"No, I did it all myself. But Mom bought the food and helped me plan the menu."

"You mean, she knew you were cooking tonight? She knew I was coming over for dinner?"

Dan glanced at her. "What do you think?"

Miranda relaxed a little. "Oh, I don't know. I guess I thought this was some big secret. Like maybe we were sneaking around and they weren't supposed to know."

"Of course they knew you were coming over." He smiled a little self-consciously and added, "Well, I *didn't* tell them I was going to use the living room, and I didn't tell them—"

"About the wine."

"Well, yeah." He hesitated. "But I wanted the meal to be special, Mandy. Really special."

"It was delicious. I told you, I'm totally impressed."

"No, I don't just mean the food. I guess I wanted . . ." His voice trailed off. He kept his eyes on the flames. "I wanted the whole night to be special. You know."

Miranda was silent.

"You look really nice tonight, Mandy. I really like that sweater. Is it new?" He reached over and put his arm around her shoulders.

She rested her head on his shoulder. "Dan, I've worn this sweater just about every day of my life."

He removed his arm and laughed awkwardly. He made her feel awkward, too. They both listened to the wind whistling around the corner of the house. "Nice weather we're having," he said suddenly.

"Now I know you're a lunatic," she said. "I thought so before, but I wasn't sure. Now it's confirmed."

Dan scowled at her. "Look, can't you help me out at all? If you won't talk about your clothes or the weather, then we'll have to talk about current events. I can't do this if you won't cooperate."

"Dan Hooton, I don't know what you're talking about! What's your problem?"

He sighed and pulled her into his arms. He pressed his lips against her hair. "Oh, damn it, Mandy. I sometimes wish you hadn't moved here just across the street, that we hadn't been friends for so long. It would be easier if I'd met you at school. Then I could ask you out for a date—just us, all alone—and not feel like I was breaking some sacred trust."

She pulled back a little, enough to see his face but not far enough that he had to let go of her. "I know what you mean," she murmured. "We know each other too well. It's like you're my brother—no, not really, but you know what I mean."

"Susannah's not the only one who wouldn't mind splitting from the pack," he said. "It's just harder for me with you." He released her and tugged a thin booklet out of his back pocket. "Here, look at this. Everything a guy could want to know. You can see how desperate I am for advice."

She took the booklet and read the title aloud, laughing. *"Every High School Boy's Guide to Social Occasions.* Oh, Dan!"

"It's from the museum—copyright 1951. Tells you how to make conversation on a date. Talk about the girl's clothes. Talk about the weather. Talk about current events." Then he grinned ruefully. "But it doesn't tell you what to do if the girl won't follow the script."

Miranda was giggling uncontrollably now; she couldn't help it. "Nice after-shave you're wearing! Nice weather we're having! What do you think about the situation in the Middle East?"

Dan grabbed her again, and they rolled back onto the floor, gasping with laughter, crazy with the sheer stupidity of social games. Finally they quieted, looked at each other, then away at the flickering fire, then back again.

Though it felt strange being so close, to hold Dan next to her this way, Miranda knew she could very easily—and very happily—get used to this new stage of their friendship. She did not have any friend she loved so well as Dan. Even Susannah, with whom she shared many interests, did not come close to being the special companion she had in Dan. Companion, and now maybe something more.

They kissed then, a long kiss that left Miranda near tears. Dan was silent a long moment after they sat apart again. Then he put more wood on the fire and poked it into flame. Miranda listened to the wind outside and thought now it sounded friendly—like the whisper of a treasured friend.

"How about a back rub?" she asked him suddenly.

He turned with a pleased smile. "Sure thing. Lie down."

"No," she told him. "You lie down this time."

His eyes lit up and he lay down obediently in front of the fire. She sat on him and pounded his shoulders.

"How about we ditch the newspaper staff?" asked Dan after a moment. "And try to get Susannah to the dance with Dave Dunlop after all? Then you and I can go together. Just us."

"You mean on a real date?" She kneaded his muscles smoothly.

"You got it." He turned over and sat up so he could see her face.

She put her hands on his shoulders. "Well . . . only if you buy me flowers." She batted her eyelashes.

He wrapped his arms around her in a happy bear hug. "Hey, what's this?" he asked, feeling the hardness of the phoenix in her skirt pocket.

She pulled it out to show him. "I love it. I always carry it with me these days."

"For luck?" he asked.

She nestled against him. "Well, it seems to be working."

Later Miranda headed home and stopped in the living room to rave to her parents about Dan's culinary expertise. She felt sleepy and did not linger long. As she climbed the stairs, her mother called, "Why not stop and say good night to Abby?"

They certainly didn't give up easily. But there was a crack of light shining under Abby's bedroom door. Miranda hesitated, wanting nothing more than to go straight to her own room and burrow in bed under the quilt and play back the wonderful evening she had just spent with Dan.

There was no answer when she knocked, and Miranda turned away, relieved. But just as she started down the hall to her room, Abby's sullen voice said, "You can come in now."

Miranda opened the door. Abby lay on the pull-out couch, her math book open on the pillows. Yet Miranda felt sure Abby had not been studying. The air seemed charged with some emotion. Sadness?

"Hi," Miranda said. "I'm home."

"Evidently."

"Well, I just wanted to say hello."

"Hello." Abby carefully adjusted the quilt on her bed.

"Dan turned out to be a fantastic cook after all."

"That's good." Abby sat looking away

from Miranda, out the dark window. The panes were frosted with ice patterns.

Miranda shrugged and moved to leave. "Well. Good night."

Abby stretched out her legs. "See you in the morning." She looked pointedly at the door, but now Miranda could not leave. She stared at the bed. Abby's math book still sat propped importantly against the pillows, but the quilt at the foot had been dislodged when Abby stretched.

Several dozen photographs—maybe more —lay uncovered by the rumpled quilt. Abby bent over them swiftly, her long, pale hair brushing them as she tugged the quilt back into place. Two bright red patches flooded her cheeks.

"What are those?"

"Get out of here, Mandy."

"Why? Let me see them. What are you hiding?" Miranda strode to the bed and pulled at the quilt.

"Get out!" hissed Abby, and Miranda knew she did not want Helen and Philip to hear their struggle. "You have no right!"

But Miranda was determined. The two girls engaged in a brief tug-of-war with the quilt, but Miranda, the stronger of the two, easily won.

She threw the quilt onto the floor and stared down at the pictures. Abby sat motionless on the bed, head bowed, face tight with anger, hostility, and something else. Fear?

In most of the photos a girl posed alone. In some she was part of a family or school group. Some photos were very old and brittle. Some were brown-and-white on thick cardboard, while others were shiny snapshots on thin paper. Still others seemed quite modern, in crisp black-and-white or in color. The most recent photo was one Miranda recognized: Abby's school picture.

As Abby swooped down to gather them up, Miranda shot out her hand and held the other girl back. She bent lower and examined the scattered photographs, then stared up at Abby in open astonishment. "Abby," she whispered. "All these"—she gestured to the pictures on the bed—"all these are the same girl. All these are pictures of *you!*"

The silence between the two girls lengthened. Miranda released her hold on Abby, but the other girl did not move. Miranda peered down at the assortment of photographs, then up at Abby again. Abby sat cross-legged on the bed, the long curtain of hair hiding her face. Her hair hung limp, swinging gently with the motion of her body as she breathed. It seemed to Miranda that the swaying hair was the only movement in the whole house, possibly in all of Garnet. Everything was oddly still. Even the snow had stopped.

"Abby?"

Abby lifted her head. Her eyes met Miranda's. The eyes, usually so dim and opaque, were now sharp and glistening with tears. Miranda flinched as if Abby had struck her, and felt relief as the light died out and Abby's eyes grew dry and empty again.

"Miranda Browne, you must be a lunatic." Abby's voice was low and calm. "Just listen to yourself. You barge in here, pry into my private things—and then say the most bizarre things. Look at these pictures!" She touched one of them. "Look how old some of these are. Look at the clothes—they're obviously before 1900. And look here." She picked out a few of the light brown-and-white pictures. "See this girl standing with the man in uniform? That's a uniform from World War I. And these here are from the twenties. And these are from the sixties—just look at the miniskirts. What do you mean, these girls are me? You don't make any sense."

"They all have your face," muttered Miranda as Abby swept the photos into a big pile and shuffled them together as if she were playing cards. "You could dress me up in all different clothes and hairstyles, too, and I'd look a little different. But my face would be the same."

Abby's voice held a note of quiet superiority. "What are you saying? Why in the world would I dress up in different costumes and have a lot of photos taken? You can see for yourself that these photos really *are* old. Look at this one—it's so brittle it's starting to crumble."

Abby's words fell like hammer blows until Miranda's head was pounding just the way it did when the piano music filled the house. Abby's quiet voice pressed on relentlessly. "Look again. The girls do look like me. I can see that, too. But family resemblances are amazing, aren't they? The Chandler women have always been small and blond, it seems. Isn't that fascinating? I guess it's something to do with genes or DNA or something."

"Or something," murmured Miranda. She went to the door. The photos could not be of Abby, she told herself. Of course not.

But they are! Somehow they really are. A leaping terror inside pressed to be released, and Miranda felt that if she stayed and listened any more to Abby's cool explanations, her fragile control would disappear. The feeling of holding panic at bay was one she had so far experienced only when she was walking alone in the dark somewhere and suddenly imagined she was being followed. Then she had to walk home quickly, but not too quickly; if she gave in to the panic she would be lost. Now, here in this room with Abby, Miranda's skin was beginning to creep with that same sense of danger.

"Sorry," Miranda said softly, backing into the hall slowly as if trying not to startle some unpredictable wild creature. "I should have realized. Family resemblances *are* weird. In fact, everyone always says I'm the exact replica of my grandmother." She turned away from the door. "Good night."

She walked slowly to her room, hands pressed against her temples, which were aching fiercely with tension. She knew those photos were of Abby—every single one of them. Yet, logically, they *could not* be.

Logically, people couldn't vanish into thin air, either. Nor could they be heard crying when they weren't even there.

Once in bed, the quilt pulled up to her chin, her eyes watching the flakes of snow illuminated by moonlight sail past her window, Miranda tried in vain to return to the safe, warm haven she had found in Dan's arms. But the memory of Abby crouched on the bed, shuffling all the old-time photographs in her small, thin hands, played through Miranda's head like a film, and she shivered.

CHAPTER NINE

IN ASSEMBLY on Wednesday the school was buzzing with excitement. The principal, stern Mr. Raphael, actually cracked a smile when he announced that ticket sales to the Valentine's Dance on Saturday night—added to the money raised by the walk-a-thon, the flea market, and the baked goods and T-shirt sales—had brought the school's total contribution to the Prindle House restoration project to over $40,000. Then he went on to say that the high school fund-raising efforts had been so successful, the Historical Society would reward students by offering them first chance at after-school and summertime jobs working on the project. Everyone cheered. His address ended with an unusual request from a man who was usually very dour: "If you haven't bought your dance tickets yet, please do so. We want to see each and every one of you right here on Saturday night, dancing as hard as you can!"

When the bell rang to send the students off to their first period classes, Susannah boogied up to Miranda's locker. "I wonder if old Raphael will be here on Saturday, dancing up a storm?"

"Well, I know I'll be." Miranda was preoccupied, but she smiled at her friend. "With Dan." She hesitated, then added, "We sort of want to make it a date."

Susannah smiled. "That's great. I'm going with Dave Dunlop. He called last night to ask me. Isn't that fantastic? Can you believe it?"

"Of course I can believe it," said Miranda. "But watch out. Sometimes he acts like he's God's gift to girls. Remind him that you're a gift, too."

"Oh, I will." Susannah hugged herself. "Hey, don't forget to come to the gym during study hall. We have to start getting the decorations up if we want everything to be ready for Saturday." She danced along beside Miranda as they made their way through the throng of students in the hallway, all chattering about the coming dance and the happy prospect of guaranteed summer jobs.

Miranda tried to feel happy and excited, too, but there was little room left inside her now for anything other than anxiety. She knew she had to see Abby's photos again, had to figure out who Abby really was. Getting the photos would not be easy, for Abby kept them inside her beaded bag and rarely left it unattended. But Miranda was determined now to take them the first chance she got.

Miranda was standing on a stepladder in the gym later that day during her study hall, a long, pink streamer looped around her shoulders, her fingertips lined with pieces of tape, when a sudden movement made her look up to the windows near the ceiling. The gymnasium was in the basement of the building, and the high, narrow windows looked out onto the playing field behind the school. In the window directly above her she could see a pair of feet in familiar bright yellow boots. On the ground next to the boots, lying in the snow against the window, was the beaded pink satchel.

Abby had geometry this period, Miranda knew—so what was she doing out in the playing field? Cutting class to go off and steal again? Miranda remained motionless, watching. After a moment the yellow boots moved out of view.

But the beaded pink bag still lay in the snow.

This might be her only chance.

Miranda stuck the streamer up as high on the wall as she could reach, then jumped off the ladder. Pulling her sweater off a bench by the door, she raced out into the hall, paying no attention to her friends' startled calls. She slipped out the door of the school and ran back into the playing field behind the building.

Miranda hurried over to the gym windows but arrived too late. The beaded bag was gone. The ridged prints from Abby's yellow boots were well defined in the snow, but Abby herself was nowhere to be seen. Miranda bit her lip, then set off across the field in Abby's tracks.

They led in a straight line, each print widely spaced as if Abby had been running. Miranda took giant steps to stay in Abby's tracks. Just at the edge of the playing field, where the woods began, Miranda stopped and stared down. A sick throbbing began in the pit of her stomach. The footprints were gone. *Again.* They had not been obliterated by more falling snow; the sky was a steely, empty blue. They simply stopped, just as they had on the sidewalk around the corner from the grocery store.

Terror is a funny thing, Miranda thought giddily, her heart pounding. Sometimes it made you want to run and hide. But sometimes it made you strong, determined to stay and fight. She strode on.

The snow on the ground was smooth and deep; only her own footprints marred the feathery white expanse. When she reached the fence surrounding the school property, she climbed right over and kept on walking. Where could Abby have gone? She couldn't fly—she *had* to be here! In spite of herself, Miranda found her eyes turning skyward.

She lost track of time as she circled around in the woods. She grew chilled. Finally she found herself back at the fence. She climbed it and hung at the top for a few minutes, peering back into the woods for a sign she might have missed. Then she looked upward again. Gray clouds hovered—more snow seemed imminent. But Abby wasn't anywhere at all. Miranda jumped down from the fence into the playing field, then gasped as a heavy hand clapped her shoulder and spun her around.

"Mr. Raphael!"

"The pleasure is mine, Miss Browne," said the principal, his voice hard-edged. "And now, if you have finished your little nature walk, perhaps you are ready to return to the seat of learning?" He was unsmiling and as grim as the gray suit he wore.

Miranda shrank from his sarcasm. She tried to explain. "Have I missed the bell? I'm sorry, but I was just following Abby. You know, she often sneaks out, and I just wanted to find out where she goes—"

Mr. Raphael, whose thick lips were beginning to look a bit blue with cold despite his gray wool suit, glowered at her. "Abby? I take it you mean Abigail Chandler?" He wheeled her around so that they faced the school building. "March back inside, Miss Browne. Straight to the office, if you please. Then you can tell me your tale."

She stumbled ahead of him along the trail she had followed. His voice close behind her acted as a prod. "You might have taken the time to think of a better story, however. Abigail is in her geometry class. It was she, in fact, who stopped by the office to report that she had seen you wandering off into the field toward the woods."

Miranda trudged on, her mind in turmoil. How could Abby be in class? Miranda had clearly seen those yellow boots, and the beaded pink bag. She had seen the running footprints deep in the snow, the prints ending impossibly.

The terror changed now. Instead of feeling strong and determined, Miranda wanted to hide. She drew the bitterly cold air into her lungs until they ached with protest, and heard herself blubbering aloud as she lumbered along in front of the principal, the words flowing out unchecked in a garbled stream. "You've got to know she's not normal, Mr. Raphael. She has powers—she can do all sorts of things. I think—I think she can *fly*. . . ."

His voice thundered behind her. "Stop your nonsense now." She pressed her hands, numb with cold, to her mouth. She had to get a hold of herself, had to contain her fear. It wouldn't help matters if he thought she were tripping out on some drug.

In Mr. Raphael's office Miranda recovered her poise and tried to apologize, but the principal halted her flow of words. "Not so fast, Miss Browne. An apology won't be enough this time, I'm afraid. I have a note here from Ms. Taylor that you've already been cited for cutting English recently. You know what that means, don't you, young lady? First offense, extra homework. Second offense, suspension from extracurricular activities for a week. Third offense, suspension from classes." He flipped through a sheaf of computer printouts on his desk, searching for her name. "Ah, yes, here you are. Second offense. This is Wednesday. So you are barred from school activities until next Wednesday morning. No clubs. No meetings—"

"But the dance—," Miranda said weakly.

"No dance." He scribbled something on a pink slip of paper and handed it to her. "I'm sorry. You heard me say this morning I hoped every student would be there. But we take a dim view of people who cut classes. Now take this paper and go to your next class. I hope you won't repeat these errors in judgment again."

Miranda left the office without a backward glance, her cheeks suffused with color. Everyone in the school knew what an intractable disciplinarian Mr. Raphael was. His word was law. Miranda's anger at being forbidden the dance and her embarrassment at having lost control in front of Mr. Raphael merged into new fury at Abby. There was something wrong about Abby, and she'd sensed it from the first day they'd met. Miranda knew without a doubt now that her family was harboring someone who was not only a liar and a thief, but something even worse. The mysterious photographs, the crying in the empty room, and the disappearing footprints in the snow were all linked in her mind as impossibilities that were possible because of Abby.

Abby was not on the school bus home.

Miranda sat next to Dan. With tears in her eyes, her mittened hands in his, she told him what had happened. "And now everything is ruined. I'm not even allowed to go to the dance."

"What a criminal you are, Miranda Browne," said Dan severely. "Good thing I've found out about your true nature. I wash my hands of you. You can forget about all the other dances, too. No April Fool's dance, no spring prom. In fact, I don't think I should even be sitting on this bus with you. . . ."

Miranda sniffed. "You don't mind?"

Dan squeezed her hands. "Hey, we can have a better time somewhere else."

"Somewhere else," she echoed. "Far away from Abby."

The bus spilled them out at the bottom of the hill, and they began the slippery hike to their houses. Miranda headed directly up the stairs when she arrived home, straight to her father's office. She tapped softly on the door and entered when he said, "If you must."

"I must, Dad," she said as he looked up from his word processor. "I'm glad you're home. I really need to talk to you."

"I've got to finish the new museum catalog by Monday," he said, and poked a few more keys. "But this sounds serious." He swiveled around to face her and lifted a pile of paper off the chair next to his desk. "Okay. Shoot."

She related as honestly as she could what had happened at school. He raised his brows when she told him of cutting two classes, being suspended from extracurricular activities, and being barred from the dance. But he did not comment until she finished. Then he leaned back in his chair and sighed. "There are a lot of things in your story, Mandy, that don't meet the eye."

"What do you mean? What eye?"

"The eye of reason." He looked at her soberly. "First of all, I'm sorry about the dance. But what can you expect if you keep cutting classes?"

"Oh, Dad, I don't keep cutting classes. Both times were just accidents. I was following Abby and just lost track of time—"

"No, that isn't true. Let's stick to what you told me. You meant to follow her today—and there's a lot I could say about *that*, Miranda Jane." When her easygoing father called her by her full name, Miranda knew he was very upset. "But you *weren't* following her after all because she was inside reporting you to Mr. Whosits for cutting. So you must have been following someone else, or—"

"Or what, Dad?" Her voice held a warning note, as if she knew what he would say next.

"Mandy, Mandy." His voice was tired. "I don't know. I'm really starting to get worried about you. Mither and I both are." He held up one hand to stave off her interruption. "Listen to me, honey. I know you don't like Abby. You've made that very clear. You know Mither and I won't force you to live with her past March if you don't like her. But I just wish you'd try a little more. It sounds to me like you and Abby are really *determined* not to get along. You're playing games with each other— setting traps. This time you tried to catch her, but she caught you instead. Maybe you'll beat her next time, but I wish you'd both just give up the games for a while and work at getting along peacefully. If you can't, even having her through March is going to be horrible for everyone. How about it? Don't you think you can give it an honest try?"

Miranda stared at a worn space on the patterned carpet. "She scares me, Dad." Should she tell him about the photographs or wait till she could show him?

He put his hand on her arm. "How do you mean? Because you think she's hiding something from us?"

"Don't you feel it, too? That her story isn't true?"

"I think Abby has had a hard life, honey. Harder, perhaps, than she wants us to know. I sense she's left bits and pieces out of her account, that's all. She may have been mixed up with a rough crowd. We have no idea how hard it's been. But thank goodness she came to Garnet instead of hiding out on the streets of Boston or New York. Runaways don't have an easy time of it out on the streets. Maybe her rudeness to you—her rough edges—are the result of her troubles."

"It's not just that." Without the photographs, he would believe nothing. She needed to have them as proof.

Proof of what? She felt very much alone in that moment. "Dad— Never mind." She would wait until she had the photos in hand.

Downstairs the piano music began again. Miranda stood up, her head beginning to pound. Hugging herself tightly, she turned to go. He could not help her, after all.

"I'm sorry about the dance, Mandy," he said as she walked out into the hall.

Miranda followed the sound of Beethoven's *Moonlight* Sonata played with furious intensity, and found Abby seated as usual at the piano. The beaded pink satchel was on the floor next to the piano bench. Miranda stood in the doorway to the music room, trying to formulate a plan to get the bag. She was taken aback when Abby lifted her hands in mid-chord and stopped playing.

Abby spoke first. "So have you come to apologize? I'm waiting."

"You'll be waiting forever, in that case. I'm waiting for *you* to apologize." They glared at each other. "And to explain. You have an awful lot of explaining to do."

"Not at all," said Abby. "I have nothing to say to you at all. You are beneath contempt. There's no reasoning with you. You're a spoiled child. Or else there's something really wrong with you."

Miranda glared at her. "I'm not the one with the problem."

"Oh, really? I just think there's something pathologically wrong with someone, Mandy, who can't keep her nose out of other people's business. Look at the way you act. You're always barging into my room hoping to catch me—at God knows what. You practically tore those photographs out of my hand the other night, you were so nosy. You cut school to track me through the streets the other week. I hate being followed. And today you went too far."

"Then it *was* you, wasn't it—crossing the playing field?"

"Maybe, maybe not," Abby taunted. "But it was I who told Mr. Raphael where to find you. I saw you wandering out there in the snow and stopped by his office on the way to class."

"And now I can't go to the dance." Miranda's voice was bitter.

"That's what you get for snooping. Besides, I had to tell him, didn't I? There you were, poor dear, off in the snow, all alone in the cold. Without a proper coat on. I thought you might be imagining things again—gone off the deep end. You can understand why I'd have to get someone to, ah, help you, can't you?" Her voice was smug, the smirk twitching at one corner of her thin mouth. "For your own good, of course. After all you've done for me."

Miranda clenched her fists at her sides, longing to hit Abby. Then she met the other girl's opaque eyes for an instant and caught a glimmer of . . . something. Something old and secret. And she had to look away.

She strove for a casual tone. "Look, how

did you make those tracks? Where did you go after you stopped walking?"

Abby's smirk was fully in place now. "I flew, of course."

The terror throbbed dully in Miranda's stomach. But she kept her voice even. "Come on. There's no way you could get back to school without leaving tracks, unless you walked backward in your own footprints."

Abby shrugged, but she was watching Miranda closely. "Well, then, I guess that's just what I did."

Miranda shook her head. "No you didn't. Because I was right behind you. I'd have seen you, you liar!"

Abby just shrugged again. "But I guess you didn't, though."

Miranda's eyes grew hard and angry. "You just *vanished*, and I want to know how."

"Shall we call it a draw, Mandy?"

Miranda stalked out of the room, expecting to hear the piano music begin again. She got as far as the kitchen, where she saw Abby's yellow boots neatly lined up on newspaper just inside the back door, when Abby's voice made her stop.

"Mandy?" Abby was right behind her, hugging the pink satchel.

Miranda stopped cold. "Now you're following me! Just leave me alone."

"When haven't I left you alone?" retorted Abby. "It's always you snooping and spying on me. But don't worry, I'll be leaving you alone. It always has to happen sooner or later. And I guess it'll be sooner, this time."

"What do you mean?" asked Miranda. The light in Abby's eyes made her uneasy.

"You can keep your precious house and parents and friends all to yourself. I won't steal them away, and I won't make you share them." Her voice was low, barely audible. "Because soon I won't be here. You won't even have to wait it out through March."

"Wait a minute, Abby!" Miranda moved toward her and looked the other girl right in the face. This was going too far. True, she *didn't* want Abby living with them, but she didn't want to live with the guilt of having driven her away, either. Or could she be threatening suicide?

Abby shifted her pink satchel. "Just wait a while longer. Then you'll never see me again." She turned to leave the room but snagged her skirt on the rough wooden edge of the door frame. As she twisted to free herself, Miranda caught a glimpse of Abby's thigh—of a red, angry welt.

"What have you done to yourself?" Miranda reached out to lift Abby's skirt.

"Leave me alone! It's nothing!"

"But you're hurt. How did this happen?" Miranda held the skirt up above Abby's knee, revealing a wound nearly an inch wide and perhaps a full three inches in length. "It looks awfully painful— Hey, it's a burn!"

"I know." And Abby pulled her skirt down abruptly. She was trembling. Hot spots of color stained her cheeks. "What were we just saying about leaving each other alone?"

"But the burn—"

"I've had it for a long time. I'll be fine."

"It doesn't look old at all. It looks like it just happened."

"It doesn't hurt much. Don't worry about me."

"But Abby—" Miranda didn't know what she intended to say, but just then Helen entered the kitchen by the back door, cold snow and wind blowing in with her. Both girls shot each other warning looks and rushed to help with the grocery bags.

As Helen disappeared into the pantry with a bag full of soup cans, Abby hissed, "Promise you won't tell her about the burn!"

"But she's a doctor. She can help you—"

"Promise me!"

Then Miranda hissed back, surprising herself. "Then you promise you'll stay through March the way it's planned. Promise you won't run away."

Abby smirked. Miranda itched to slap her.

CHAPTER
TEN

ON SATURDAY NIGHT when most of the other high school students were dancing in the gym, Miranda and Dan sat across from each other at The Sassy Café on Main Street. Dan's father had dropped them off at the café, where Dan had reserved a quiet corner table. They ordered garlic breadsticks as an appetizer and munched companionably while Dan told Miranda about the special project he'd decided to do for his photography class.

"Since we're working on the Prindle House anyway, I thought I'd do a photo essay about it—you know, give the history and then show the different stages of renovation," he explained. "The Historical Society has all sorts of records and stuff I bet they'd let me see."

"Sounds good," said Miranda. "I bet you'll get an A."

Then their meals arrived. "This is much better than being at that stupid dance," said Miranda as she bit into her juicy burger. She reflected that although she and Dan had shared many picnics, school lunches, and family dinners, the two of them had never been out to dinner alone.

Dan nodded as he sipped his chocolate milkshake. Then he wiped his mouth and added, "But I *am* sorry I won't get to hold you in my arms for three hours!"

"If we were dancing, you wouldn't be holding me anyway," Miranda pointed out. "Not unless you've suddenly learned how to waltz or something." She remembered what Abby had said about kids today not knowing how to dance, jumping around, never touching. She gazed at him across the table, liking the way his dark hair just touched the collar of his flannel shirt and the way his lips curved around the straw. She added boldly, "But maybe we can arrange something anyway."

"Maybe a little private waltz?"

"Yeah, something like that." She looked down and began eating again.

They finished their meal and Dan paid, pushing aside Miranda's offer to split the bill. "My pamphlet says the boy *always* has to pay."

"That was in 1951," she reminded him.

"Maybe boys had more money then or something."

"Next time," he said. "We can take turns."

"That's a good plan," she said, taking his hand as they left The Sassy Café, glad there would be more dates like this, just the two of them.

They walked through the quiet, snow-blanketed streets. He tucked both their hands into the pocket of his coat. They passed the high school, where lights burned brightly. When some students opened the doors to the gymnasium and hurried across the parking lot, music spilled out with them. But when the doors swung shut again, the music disappeared. "Who needs it?" asked Dan, and he pulled Miranda into his arms. "Listen carefully," he whispered into Miranda's hood. "I think I hear the strains of a waltz. Don't you?"

She pulled the little statue of the phoenix from her pocket and blew its clear note into the air. "Absolutely."

"You still have that thing?" He grinned.

She nodded. "I told you, it's my good luck charm. I love it." She couldn't explain any better than that why she kept the phoenix with her now all the time. She didn't really know why herself.

In the street lamp light, needing no music

at all, they whirled across the parking lot. Then they walked on across town to the common, where they slid on the frozen pond, shrieking with laughter until they both grew tired. "How about stopping for ice cream sundaes before we head back up the hill?" asked Miranda. "This time it can be my treat."

"Sounds good to me," said Dan, and they walked with their arms around each other back to Main Street.

Later, back on Miranda's front porch, they kissed good night. Then Miranda let herself inside and climbed the stairs to her room, filled with happiness. She thought about Dan as she slipped into her flannel nightgown and brushed her teeth, about how comfortable and easy it was to be with him, and yet how exciting at the same time. She peeked into her parents' bedroom to say good night.

They were both reading in bed. "Did you have a good time?" asked her father.

"Just look at you glow!" said her mother. "I guess you *did* have fun, dance or no dance."

"We danced in the snow," Miranda told them. "It was *wonderful*."

Then she froze, motionless at the side of their bed. The sound of crying, low, dark, and full of a fearful grief filtered into the room. *Abby.*

Miranda held her breath, listening. She looked at her parents. Philip was reading again. Helen was looking at her with concern.

"What is it, honey?" Helen asked.

"You don't hear this?" Miranda headed for the door, fear thumping in her stomach, then ran down the hall to Abby's room. She threw open the door. Cries of lamentation, raw and deep, filled the room, but Abby was not there.

Determined to end the mystery, Miranda pressed back her terror and crossed the room to fling open the closet door. Abby's new clothes hung neatly on hangers, her beaded bag lay on the floor, and Helen's metal file cabinet filled the rest of the space.

No Abby.

Miranda grabbed the satchel. She turned and pelted down the hallway as fast as she could. She peeked into the bathroom and into her father's study, then darted back into her parents' room. This time she would make them believe her.

"Mandy, my goodness!" Philip slid out of bed and reached for his robe.

"What's wrong?" demanded Helen.

Miranda dumped the beaded bag onto their bed. "It's just like before—Abby's not in her room, and there's all this crying, and there's something horribly wrong. But this time I can prove it to you!" She fumbled with the clasp on Abby's bag, but broke off as the crying ceased and the toilet flushed in the bathroom across the hall.

Then Abby walked past the open door to the master bedroom.

"Abby!" yelled Miranda, abandoning the satchel. "Wait!"

"What have I done now?" Abby stopped in the doorway. She stared at the bed. "How dare you take my things?"

Philip glanced at Miranda. "Mandy thought she heard you crying again. And you weren't in your room."

"I was in the bathroom," Abby said flatly. "And I wasn't crying." She reached for the beaded bag.

Miranda narrowed her eyes. "You were not in the bathroom! I looked there."

No one could stare more coldly than Abby, and she turned that opaque gaze on Miranda now. "Can't I go to the bathroom around here without you going into hysterics?"

"I wasn't the one in hysterics—you were! Do you think I'm deaf?"

"I think you're out of your mind, Miranda Browne. That's what I think."

Helen ran her fingers through her hair. "Girls, girls." She exchanged an anxious glance with Philip.

Miranda gritted her teeth. "Show them the photos, then," she hissed. "Show them how I'm out of my mind."

Abby clutched her satchel to her chest. "I don't know what you're talking about. Just keep out of my stuff, I'm warning you."

"Are you threatening me?" cried Miranda.

Abby looked away. "I'm going back to bed."

"Wait a second," said Helen. "What photos, Mandy? What do you mean?"

Abby answered before Miranda had a chance to explain. "Photos of my family, that's what. She's been snooping again. She stole my bag right out of my room."

"Mandy, really. Don't you think you owe Abby an apology?" Helen pursed her lips.

"Mither," begged Miranda. "Just take a look at her pictures."

"I'll wait until Abby wants to share them," said Helen firmly. "And so, I think, should you."

Philip nodded in agreement. "What I think is that it's bedtime," he said. Abby stalked away without another word. Philip turned to Miranda. "Come on, Mandy. March will be here soon." He kissed the top of her head.

She spun on her heels and walked out. She heard their low voices murmuring even after their door had closed. Sullenly, she went into the bathroom. She felt flushed and trembly, as if she were coming down with the flu. She splashed cool water over her face, then stared into the mirror a long time, trying to sort out what was going on. She wanted desperately to be with Dan. Was it too late to call him? At least he would listen to her. She decided she would use the phone downstairs. Finally, feeling calmer, she returned to her bedroom to get her robe.

Abby was sitting cross-legged in the center of her bed.

"Get out," Miranda snapped. "Out."

"Listen—I need to talk to you," began Abby in a low voice. "I—"

"I said, get out."

"Please, Mandy." Abby's voice was a whisper, and she bent her head forward so that the curtain of pale hair hid her face.

Miranda grabbed her bathrobe and left the bedroom. She hurried down the hall and down the stairs. Abby trailed along behind her. "Please," Abby persisted. "I don't want your parents to hear. But I have to tell you you were right. I *wasn't* in the bathroom at all. And I *was* crying."

"Of course I was right," snapped Miranda.

"Ssh, not so loud," whispered Abby, glancing up the stairs. She wiped her eyes on her sleeve. "You've been right all along. But why do you think your parents never heard anything?"

"I don't know," hissed Miranda. "And there isn't much point asking you to explain, is there?" She stalked through the dining room into the kitchen and closed the swinging door in Abby's face.

Abby swung the door open and followed Miranda into the kitchen. "I need to tell you."

Miranda put her hands on her hips. "You'll explain everything? The disappearances? The weird photos? All the yowling?" She was shaking as she faced Abby but made her voice loud and hard. She didn't want the other girl to know how afraid she felt.

"Yes. Everything. I'll tell you because of the crying, Mandy. Because you hear me when no one else in the world can." Abby sank into a chair at the round table.

Miranda sat down across from her. "Go on. This had better be good."

Abby cupped her chin in her hands and smiled slightly over at Miranda. It was a real smile, the first Miranda had seen from her, without a single trace of smugness. Abby hooked her feet around the legs of the chair and spread her hands on the tabletop. "I really don't know how to tell you this. There have been so few people I've ever been able to talk to, and only a few have ever really believed me. But you're different somehow. Special."

"I'm honored," said Miranda sarcastically. But now she was giving Abby her full attention.

Abby sighed and glanced at the closed kitchen door. "Will you listen?"

"Get on with it." Miranda vowed to herself that she wouldn't believe a word, whatever Abby said.

"I'm not who you think I am," Abby began slowly. "I'm not what I said I was. . . ." And despite herself, Miranda found herself listening intently, and her skin felt tingly at the back of her neck.

"Because you have heard my crying, maybe you can understand how it is with me, why I have to pretend to be . . ."

"To be what?"

"To be a normal teenage girl."

Miranda almost opened her mouth to point

out she didn't find Abby normal at all, but the tingly sensation remained with her and she kept silent.

"I have to pretend all the time," Abby said softly. "Not only that, I have to pretend different things at different times. I must be on guard constantly, always watching to make sure what I say is appropriate to the place and the people I'm with. For the *time*. Do you see?"

"Nope."

Abby shifted in her chair and stretched her hand across the table toward Miranda. "Look—how old are you?"

"You know I'm fifteen. Just like you."

"No, I told you I was fifteen, but I'm not. I'm really only thirteen. That is, I mean, I *was* thirteen. . . ."

"Okay, so you lied about your age. But what's that got to do with crying? Or the photos?"

Abby rubbed her fingers through her hair. "When were you born, Mandy? What year?"

Miranda told her. "But so what?"

"So, listen to me. I was born in 1680."

Miranda snorted. "Well now, ain't that amazing!" She stood up. "Thanks for being so honest with me, Abby. I really appreciate it." She glanced at the clock on the wall and put her hands on her hips. "And now it's really too late for me to call Dan, so I'm going up to bed."

Abby jumped up. "You said you'd listen! You're not even paying attention!"

"How stupid do you think I am?" shouted Miranda, furious that Abby was still making fun of her. She didn't care whether her parents heard them or not. "You are the biggest liar I've ever met in my life! Why should I listen to you?" She started out of the room.

"Because," whispered Abby, and suddenly she was sobbing. The sound was so familiar that Miranda stopped and turned back. "Because *you* heard me. Don't you see? I wasn't there. I wasn't in the room at all, just like you said. I was where no one has ever heard me, where no one could have heard me—except for some-one who was somehow very sensitive. That's why I have to make you listen." Standing there with her pale hair flowing over her shoulders and her arms outstretched, Abby looked like a little lost girl, a girl much younger than fifteen—or even thirteen, if that were her true age.

"Believe me, Mandy, I don't like you any better than you like me. I've met a lot of girls much nicer than you—I've lived with girls much more friendly than you. But you are the only one—the only one *ever*—who might be able to help me."

Miranda sank slowly back into her chair. "Okay, go on," she said grudgingly.

Abby hitched her chair closer and leaned toward Miranda. Her voice was low, confiding. "I was born in 1680. Honest." She shrugged. "Why in the world should I make it up?"

Miranda did not answer. She had no idea why Abby did anything.

"I lived in Garnet with my parents and my sisters—I had two sisters, named Constance and Faith. I had a brother, too, named Thomas, who was older and married. I was hoping to get married myself in another few years, when I turned sixteen." She traced the woodgrain in the tabletop. "It was different then. People got married earlier, you know."

"You lived in Garnet?" A dozen questions were tumbling through Miranda's head, but this was the only one she could articulate. "You lived right here in *Puritan* times? You expect me to believe this?"

"It was different here then. You wouldn't know the place. Oh, Mandy, it was beautiful. And we were so happy, William and I." Abby's eyes were starry. "We had fallen in love. Maybe we were young, but we wanted to be together

every second. It was like—well, sort of like
what I see with you and Dan. We were special
to each other. Vital to each other."

None of this made sense. But when Abby's
voice trailed away, Miranda found herself eager
for further details, almost as if she believed what
Abby was telling her. "Go on."

"There was—an accident. A fire."

"A fire? And what happened?"

"The roof of our house collapsed. We were
inside at the time. It was dinnertime, and Wil-
liam was there, too." She drew a ragged breath.
"You see? Not everything I told you was a lie.
I said my parents died in a fire, and they did.
My sisters and William were killed, too."

Miranda leaned across the space separating
them. Of course no part of this wild tale could
be true; still, she had to ask. "But you, Abby?
You got out."

"Well," she said softly. "Not exactly."

CHAPTER
ELEVEN

MIRANDA FELT GOOSE BUMPS rise on the backs of her arms. "Abby, are you trying to tell me you're a ghost?"

"I don't know what I am."

"I don't believe a word of it." Miranda shook her head. "This is crazy."

"I swear to you it's the absolute truth."

"This is just another way to make me look stupid. Or to get my parents to send me off to a locked ward. When I tell them this story—that'll be it. You can be their only child."

"Oh, Mandy." Abby reached out a tentative hand and touched Miranda's arm. "I know I can't expect you to trust me, but I wish you'd try. The fact that you could hear me crying when I wasn't here *means* something. It must."

"Means what?" Miranda stared at her.

Abby looked around the kitchen. Then she whispered, "I think you're meant to save me."

"Save you how?"

"I don't know how. But I sure know I need help." Now Abby's voice cracked with tears. "There must be something you can do."

Miranda got up and went to the refrigerator. She felt confused. Was Abby still lying—or not? How could she *not* be lying? Miranda opened the door and peered inside, then brought out a big chunk of cheddar cheese. She crossed to the bread bin and found some rye bread. She brought these to the table, then set out plates and knives. Abby watched without a word, her eyes pleading. "Okay," Miranda said, sitting back down. "Tell me what you want me to do." The sight of desperate hope in Abby's strange, cloudy eyes both frightened and compelled her.

"I want to be with my family again," Abby said simply. "I want to be back with them, and live with them, and grow up and marry William. That's all."

"That's all? Sure you don't want to throw in a couple million bucks?" She shook her head and unwrapped the cheese. "You're telling me your family died in a fire—oh, about three hundred years ago. And yet somehow you're here. But you want to go back to them. What do you think I am—magic?"

"Maybe you are. After all, you heard me crying. I just want to be back with my family. Any way you can arrange it."

Miranda shook her head again. She made herself a cheese sandwich and shoved the bread over to Abby. "Look, let's start with this crying." She frowned at Abby. She needed to get things straight. She needed time to think about what Abby was telling her. None of it made any sense. All of it was impossible. And yet . . . She had long felt that Abby was not like other girls. She had long suspected Abby of harboring some deep secret. These revelations were puzzling but also strangely comforting. Miranda wanted her parents to hear this. She had *not* been imagining things.

Abby smiled her lopsided smile and shifted in her chair. She reached for the bread but didn't make a sandwich. Instead she sat there rolling the dough into little balls. "Whenever you hear me crying," she began softly, "I'm back in Garnet just after it happened. Somehow just by wishing it so much, I can go back. I'm at my house—what's left after the fire. My mother and father are dead in the ruins. My sisters, too, and William. I think of the ways I could have saved them all, if only I had noticed when the sparks first flew up the chimney and ignited the roof. I could have warned them, and no one would have died. I just stand there and cry."

She swept the little bread pellets into her hand and looked at them. "I don't know why I didn't die in the fire along with the others, but I figure I must have been spared for a reason. I think I know what to do—but I don't know how to do it. I think maybe I need to travel back farther in time, to before the fire happened so I can warn them." She searched Miranda's face. "Can you understand how hard it is for me? I wish so hard, and yet I can't get back far enough to save them. Again and again I feel myself pulled back to the ruin. It's as if I have to try, try, and keep trying. Yet every time I go back, I'm absolutely powerless. It's like I'm not wholly there. No one can see me. I wander around, but can't really do anything—it's as if . . ." Her voice trailed off.

"As if you're a ghost," murmured Miranda. She still didn't really understand what Abby was telling her. Why wasn't Abby killed in the fire? How could she be alive *now*? How was it possible to travel back in time to a Garnet that hadn't existed for centuries? Miranda had so many questions, she didn't know where to start. "So what about all those photos?" she finally asked. "Where do they come into this?"

Abby was gazing down at the bread balls in her palm. Miranda reached over and shook her arm. "What about them? They really are of you, aren't they? Not of your ancestors at all."

Abby seemed to make an effort to return from the memory of that burned house, those charred remains of her family. She dropped the little balls and dragged her fingers through her long hair. "Oh, yes. They're all of me. You were absolutely right, and I'm sorry I lied to you."

Again Miranda felt some of the tentacles of an earlier fear loosen around her heart. "But how?" she asked. "There were photos taken around the turn of the century. There were photos from before you were born—I mean—"

Abby's lips curved. "You're starting to get it, I think." There was a trace of her former derisiveness in her tone. "Think, Mandy. I told you I was born in 1680, right? And here I am now. Old, right? Very old. Older than anybody." Her shoulders sagged. "I've been around forever, practically, and in that long a time you can collect quite a few mementos. I've never been able to stay in one place for long, but I can, at least, carry a few things with me.

Photos are one way I can remember some of what happens as the years go by. I'll show you my pictures, all of them, I promise."

"Go get them," Miranda said urgently. "Right now."

"Not now. I'm exhausted, and so are you. How many shocks do you think you can absorb in one night?"

"What's this sudden concern for my health?"

"I know you'll want to show Dan, too, so we'll wait till we're all together. Tomorrow."

Miranda's eyes felt gritty. She rubbed them, then sat looking at Abby, trying to decide whether anything she had heard tonight was real. It was true, though, that she wanted Dan to know what was going on.

Abby stood up. Her hair was a stream of silver in the moonlight through the kitchen window. "You can wait," she said. Her mocking grin flashed briefly, but her words were gentle. "I've learned a lot about waiting. You get good at it—when you have all the time in the world."

After Abby left the kitchen, Miranda sat staring at the tabletop until, finally, she roused herself and went up to bed. But she couldn't sleep. Abby's strange story left her shivering, no matter how many blankets she piled onto her bed. Finally she went to the linen closet in the hall and rummaged around till she found the old, red hot-water bottle. She took it into the bathroom and filled it with hot water. She returned to bed and hugged the rubber bottle to her chest, closing her eyes as its warmth seeped through her. It seemed ages ago that she and Dan had danced in the snow. Ages since they had kissed good night on the porch. Ages and ages and ages . . .

Finally her eyes closed, and she fell into a confusing dream in which she wandered the streets of Garnet, looking for Abby. Every time she thought she'd found her, Abby darted around a corner, pale hair flashing, and was gone again.

Miranda woke up feeling groggy and leaden. But as she rubbed her eyes, memory returned, and she jumped out of bed with sudden energy and pulled on her clothes. She would call and tell Dan to come over right away. They would make Abby show them the photos before breakfast.

But breakfast was already underway when Miranda ran downstairs. She tried several times over breakfast to catch Abby's eye without success. Helen and Philip were outlining their battle plan for a day of spring cleaning. It consisted of chores and more chores. Miranda tried to point out that it wasn't anywhere near spring yet, but her mother handed her a list of jobs. "Think positive," Helen said. "We'll get a head start."

There was no time to call Dan. No private moment to talk to Abby. As they drove to the shopping center in Lexington on a myriad of errands, Abby chatted brightly with Helen and Philip, but did not once look at Miranda in any other than her usual cursory way. When they returned home for lunch, Virginia Hooton phoned to invite the Brownes and Abby over for pizza that evening. Helen accepted with pleasure. Then she sent Miranda to clean the attic.

"Can't Abby help?" Miranda asked. She felt she would burst with wanting to talk.

"Let's keep the peace and have you work separately," suggested Philip on his way to the basement with the toolbox. "Abby can help me build a wine rack."

"No, really. I'd like her help," begged Miranda.

And Abby added, "I'll help her. I don't mind."

Helen shrugged. "All right. But no fighting."

Miranda led the way upstairs. Abby followed, carrying a broom and dustpan. The attic was cold and dark, lit only by the single bulb dangling from the low ceiling. The room stretched the whole length of the house, its corners shadowed and feathery with cobwebs. The center of the big room was full of the Brownes' suitcases, boxes of old china and books, trunks of summer clothes in storage, and crates of Christmas decorations. Miranda's job was to sweep up the dust.

"This shouldn't take long," Abby said, and began sweeping by the long, low windows. Miranda blocked her path.

"What are you doing?"

Abby widened her eyes. "Sweeping!"

"I mean, why are you ignoring me?"

"I'm not ignoring you."

"Yes, you are. You're avoiding me—as if we never talked last night."

Abby's lips curved in a smile. "Oh, we talked. But I can't look at you without wanting to tell you about everything—so I thought I'd better stay busy until tonight when we're over at Dan's."

Miranda breathed a big sigh of relief. She realized only then how afraid she was that Abby would laugh scornfully and say Miranda was just imagining things again. "You'll bring the photos when we go over for pizza?"

"Absolutely." Abby knelt to sweep dirt into the dustpan, then glanced up at Miranda. "If you're willing to help me."

"I want to try."

Abby continued sweeping. Dust rose in clouds in the attic and made both girls cough. "You're making a big promise, I have to warn you. Because I'm really very selfish. My problem occupies all my time, all my energy. I know you have your life to lead. You have to go to school and learn things, and take tests, and follow the rules. You have to have friends—and boyfriends. And do all sorts of things. But it's hard for me to concentrate on anything but myself. Playing the piano is about the only way I can keep myself here—in this time. Otherwise I find myself being drawn back, trying to get to my family again." She looked at Miranda imploringly. "So when you say you want to help me, I'm worried you don't know what I mean. I need you to immerse yourself in my problem until we can find a way out of it. I'm afraid—I'm afraid you won't have the time and energy to help me, because there are too many other things you need to do with your life."

"But—but don't you want to do things,

too?" asked Miranda. She reached for the broom. "Go to school, have friends, learn things?"

Abby shook her head impatiently. "I've done all that already." She glanced toward the stairs as if afraid Helen or Philip would come up. "I've done it all, again and again. Parties, dates, school, teenage stuff—I was doing it all before you were ever born. Before your parents were born." She held the dustpan for Miranda. "I don't think I can ever make anybody understand what it's like for me."

"But you never get any older," murmured Miranda wonderingly. "How lucky."

Abby stared at her. "Lucky?" she cried. "Oh, you don't know what you're saying. I'm thirteen in body—maybe thirteen at heart— but I've been around for so many years longer than that. I've worked on farms, in mills, in factories. I've had friends killed in battle. I've traveled and moved a hundred times or more. Think, Mandy. You'll grow up. You'll graduate from high school, you'll date people, you'll go to college, probably. You'll have a career. Maybe you'll get married and have children. And I'll always be old enough to be the baby-sitter!" Her voice was bitter. "Most importantly, you'll become an adult, and you'll understand things from an adult point of view. . . . Oh, Mandy, don't you see? I've lived dozens of lives, but I've been thirteen for almost three hundred years. I'm afraid I'll be thirteen forever!"

Miranda practically flew across the road to Dan's house that evening, but Abby dragged her feet. "As much as I need your help, this is going to be hard," she told Miranda. "I've learned from long experience not to tell. He's not going to believe a word I say."

"He'll want to help you, too."

"You might find yourself losing a boy-friend, Mandy. He'll think we're both insane."

"He'll see the pictures," Miranda said. "Don't they say a picture is worth a thousand words?"

She climbed the steps to the Hootons' front porch and rang the bell. Abby stood clenching and unclenching her mittened hands while they waited. The photographs were in a large manila envelope tucked under her arm. She seemed very small in her big denim jacket and bright yellow boots. Virginia Hooton opened the door and smiled to see the girls. "You're a little early for dinner," she greeted them, "but come on in."

They stepped inside the foyer, and Miranda introduced Abby. She explained they wanted to speak to Dan. Mrs. Hooton shook Abby's hand and said how nice it was to meet her. And, before Miranda's eyes, Abby seemed to shrug off her little-girl shyness and metamorphose into a poised young woman. She lifted her head and smiled graciously and said how pleased she was to have been invited with the Brownes. She admired the Hootons' house, and said she was looking forward to the museum tour someday soon. Mrs. Hooton and Abby walked together through the dining room while Miranda followed. She was impressed by Abby's unexpected social graces. But perhaps in nearly three hundred years even the rudest girl could learn a few manners to put on when it pleased her.

Dan and Buddy were sitting at the kitchen table playing cards. Ed Hooton waved at the girls from a desk in the corner of the big, warm room, where he was talking on the telephone.

"Hooray, it's time for pizza!" cried Buddy.

"Not yet," Miranda told him. "We're early because we need to talk to Dan. Alone."

"No fair," wailed Buddy. "He's teaching me how to play Clock Solitaire."

Abby pulled out a chair and sat down. She put the envelope on her lap. "Go ahead and finish," she said. "Take your time. We're in no hurry."

"Yes, we are," countered Miranda.

Dan looked from one girl to the other. "How about I finish showing him—fast? Then we can go upstairs. If it's really so important."

"It's hugely important," said Miranda. At the same time Abby assured him, "Oh, it can wait."

Buddy learned to lay the cards out in a circle of twelve piles with one pile in the middle. Dan showed him how to turn the cards over, hoping against hope not to turn up a king. "Four kings and you've lost," he warned Buddy, turning over another card. "Oops—see? I've just lost. Now you can try it on your own while we go upstairs."

"Stay and show me again," begged Buddy.

"Sorry, Buddy," Miranda told him. "But it's urgent."

"Oh, I don't know," said Abby, reluctant to follow them out of the kitchen. "I could just stay here with him while you two go—"

"Abby!" Miranda put her hands on her hips. Dan looked on, mystified.

"Oh, all *right*." Abby trailed behind them as Miranda led the way upstairs to Dan's room.

Dan sprawled across his bed. Miranda

settled herself next to him, while Abby sat as primly as was possible in the big, soft beanbag chair, smoothing her hands nervously over the manila envelope.

"So?" began Dan. "What's up?"

CHAPTER
TWELVE

MIRANDA HESITATED only a moment. Then she took a deep breath and began. "Abby has told me her secret. And we want you to know it, too."

Abby put her hands to her face, her cheeks pink.

"Go on," invited Dan, and he pulled a pillow under his head. "What's the big deal?"

That was one of the things about Dan that Miranda loved. He was a great listener. He wasn't thinking that soon it would be his turn to talk; he put himself aside. He wanted to hear. He seldom interrupted, and his mind never wandered.

Abby ducked her head, pale hair swinging. She looked small and childlike again, all sophistication erased. So Miranda began telling

Dan about Abby's crying the night before, about their talk in the kitchen, about everything Abby had told her. Then Miranda sat back to wait for Dan's response.

It was slow in coming. He always mulled things over before speaking, but this time it was a full three minutes, during which Miranda sat motionless, gazing out at the new snow drifting silently past the window. Abby was curled sideways in the beanbag chair, resting her head on its smooth back. Her hair shielded her face.

Finally, Dan spoke. "*Wow*. What else can I say?"

"You can say what you think it's all about," Miranda told him.

He turned to look at Abby's still, small form in the brown chair. "Poor Abby. We'll have to think of how to help you."

Abby sat up slowly, her eyes wide. Miranda threw her arms around him, laughing. "You're great, Dan Hooton. Do you know that? Who else would have listened to me without cracking jokes? Who else would have believed it? See, Abby? Wasn't I right? Who else would have believed us?"

Dan gently removed her arms. "Hold on just a second. I said we needed to help. That isn't quite the same as believing the whole story." He ran his hand through Miranda's curls. "But I believe you both believe it's true. So that's a start. I think we need to find out if it could possibly be true or if—and you have to admit this is more likely—Abby is, well, you know . . . confused."

"You mean crazy," muttered Abby. "I knew it. It's better to keep quiet."

Miranda shook her head. "Come on, show him the pictures, Abby."

When Abby didn't move, Miranda went over and removed the envelope from her unresisting hand. She was so eager to see them herself that her hand shook as she dumped the contents onto Dan's bed: all the old, yellowed photographs, newspaper clippings, recent snapshots, all separated into neat piles and tied with faded satin ribbons. "Take a look," she invited.

Dan fingered the pile of sepia-tone photos backed on cardboard. "What are these? How old are they? They look like they ought to be in a museum, or at least an album."

Abby joined them on the bed. "If you're going to see them, I want you to see them in order." She pawed through the carefully sorted stacks and selected one. She untied the ribbon slowly.

"Here," she said, and lay one photograph

on the bed. Miranda and Dan leaned forward to see. "This was the first photo ever made of me. It is me—I swear it."

Miranda stared at the dingy brown cardboard. Abby's face—and only the face was familiar—peered out at the camera from a bundle of shawls. Her body appeared to be swathed in voluminous layers of cloth. But despite the strange garments, Miranda recognized the spark in the girl's pale eyes and the familiar quirky uplift of one corner of the small mouth. A leather trunk stood at her feet. A spindly table at her side held a candle and a book. Miranda turned the photograph over gingerly, afraid it might crumble. She read aloud the dim writing penned on the back: *Abby, 1852.*

Miranda dropped the cardboard. Hearing Abby's story, telling it to Dan—none of that had prepared her for the wings of panic now fluttering somewhere deep inside.

Abby held up the next photograph by one brittle corner. "That first one was taken when I worked as a maid for the Longridge family in Boston. This next one was taken a few years later by another family I lived with—in New York."

This photograph showed Abby posed by a graceful curving staircase. She was dressed lavishly in a ruffled gown. The skirts stood out

stiffly, held high by hoops, and in her hand she
carried an open fan.

"The dress was deep green and the fan had
a hunting scene on it," murmured Abby. "They
bought the stuff for their daughter's entrance
into society because they wanted me to look
nice, too. I was living with the Petersons as a
companion for Deborah, who was sort of
sickly. They treated me like another daughter.
The mother even promised I would have a
coming-out ball myself when I was old
enough—but of course I couldn't stay with
them that long."

Miranda turned over the photograph and
read the faded lettering: *Abigail, age sixteen.
The New York Cotillion, 1856.* "But you aren't
sixteen," she protested weakly.

"No. I've always had to lie—just to get by.
Sometimes it's hard to keep track of the stories.
Who am I this time? How old am I? What
background have I concocted for myself? It's
like, I don't know, being a spider or something.
Spinning webs around me for protection. But
they're sticky, too. And they get torn down
easily." She sucked on her bottom lip, looking
at the photos. "Anyway, it's hard to get work
if I tell my true age. It's bad enough being so
small."

"What do you mean, you couldn't stay

with the Petersons long?" Dan asked. "Why couldn't you?"

"I always have to move on because I never get any older. Sooner or later, people notice. I have to find another place to live before they get suspicious."

Dan frowned. "But why couldn't you stay with these families anyway? And how did you find them in the first place? And where did you go when you left them—" He reached for the photo Miranda was holding and stared at it. "It's all so bizarre."

"But you have to believe the story now, don't you?" pressed Miranda. "You can't look at these things and not believe."

Abby looked hurt. "You're right about one thing—it *is* bizarre. *I'm* bizarre. I thought of joining a circus sideshow once, just to find a permanent home. You know: Girl Wonder! Never Ages!"

"Sorry, Abby," said Dan softly. He was nearly as pale as Abby herself as he studied the photographs. "It's just hard to believe. I mean, the whole thing. Your story—and these pictures as proof. The photos *could* be fakes, you know." He looked earnestly at Miranda. "They seem old and all that, but even age could probably be faked with special techniques."

"I don't think they're fakes," maintained Miranda.

"Yeah? But Abby's a self-confessed liar. Why should this story be any more true than any other story she's told over the years?"

"Over the years, Dan? Listen to yourself. Either you believe Abby's as old as she says she is, or you don't. The only reason she's told so many lies is because she's had to cope." Miranda glowered at him. "I think you're being horrible. Think of how awful it is for Abby to tell the truth for once and have no one believe her."

"Well, at least she's got you in her corner now," said Dan coolly. "And that was no easy conquest."

They stared at each other. "Truth is stranger than fiction," Miranda told him, moving away so their arms were no longer touching. "Haven't you heard that saying before?" *We're fighting*, she thought. *I can't believe it.*

They faced each other on the bed, frowning. Miranda glanced over to see how Abby was reacting, then screamed and clutched Dan's arm.

Abby had vanished. She had been sitting in the beanbag chair only a moment before. She had not passed the bed to leave the room. And there was no other way out.

Dan leapt off the bed in a panic. "Where'd she go? Abby!" He picked up the beanbag chair, dropped it again, ran to the window and looked out, then turned to Miranda with terror in his eyes. She sat motionless on the bed, tense and waiting.

Suddenly the air in the room seemed to change. It felt denser for an instant, as if atoms were somehow rearranging themselves. And then Abby was there again, back in the beanbag chair.

"Proof," Abby said softly. "All I have to do is wish to be back at the ruin, and I'm there."

"Oh, Abby." Miranda's heart was beating hard, as if she had been running. She regarded Abby with awe.

"I can't blame anybody for doubting me," Abby continued. "But seeing is believing."

"I believe you," whispered Dan. "I believe you. Just don't—don't do that again."

Miranda reached for Dan's hand and held it tightly.

"I promise I won't—at least not without warning you. But listen, let me tell you the whole story, just as I remember it," Abby offered. She shuffled thoughtfully through the stacks of pictures as Miranda and Dan recovered themselves and settled back on the bed together. She had their undivided attention.

"I guess I have to start with the fire at my house," Abby began. Her voice was gentle, as if she were sorry for having frightened them and didn't want to do it again. "It was a hot night in July, in 1693. Right here in Garnet. I was thirteen—almost fourteen, just like I am now. We were having a special dinner at my house for William, who was turning sixteen. He lived next door. Our own house was small, but with a large garden. We had chickens and geese. There were my father and mother, and my sisters, Constance and Faith. Our brother, Thomas, wasn't there that night." She stared out at the falling snow.

"Anyway—it was awfully hot and dry that summer, but even so, we always kept the fire going—that was the only way to heat water or to cook, you know. The roof caught fire while we were eating dinner. It flared up so suddenly—and it just fell in on us. I was at the table talking to William and suddenly everything was chaos. I could hear my mother and my sisters screaming—and I could hear my father shouting. I couldn't see anything in the smoke. It was all around me. I couldn't breathe.

I felt something burn my leg—and then, I don't remember what happened. Somehow I was out of the house. The smoke was clearing. Everything was all in ruins. Men were everywhere with buckets of water trying to keep sparks from jumping over to the Prindles' place—"

"The *Prindle* House?" interrupted Miranda in surprise.

"That's right—your same Prindle House." A fleeting smile lifted the corners of Abby's mouth. "Well, nearly the same. It may be the oldest house in Garnet now, but it wasn't then. William's father had built it only the year before."

"What happened next?" ventured Dan. "Did you go to the men?"

"Of course," said Abby, resuming her tale. "I saw my brother Thomas and ran to him. I grabbed his arm—I was crying, but he didn't see me! He didn't feel me there at all. I ran all around, trying to make someone hear me, but it was like I wasn't even there. William's father came along, and another neighbor, but they couldn't see me, either. I thought—I thought I must have died after all. I must have become a ghost."

Miranda nestled against Dan. She felt in need of comforting.

"I waited there until the men had every spark out," Abby continued in a low voice. "And when they left, I tried to follow—but I couldn't. I couldn't leave the site of my house. It was as if—I can't explain it. As if there were a wall of wind holding me back. I tried my hardest to press through the wall and felt myself caught up in—I don't know what it was—a kind of whirlwind or something. I couldn't see, I couldn't hear anything but roaring—and I thought, well, if I hadn't died already, this was surely the end." She smoothed her palm over the manila envelope. "But it wasn't the end. Because when the wind stopped, there I was, standing in a field next to the Prindle House. A *field*, don't you see? Where there hadn't been any field before because my house stood there."

Miranda didn't see at all. She just sat with her hand in Dan's and waited, and Abby continued after a moment of silence. "The field was covered with patches of snow, and I was shivering, wearing only my summer dress. Seconds before it had been summer. Now I was freezing. There was no sign of my house at all—no rubble, no ash. Just grass and snow. I started walking toward the Prindle House, and then I noticed it looked different. It was bigger. There was a porch and a whole other wing.

But what was I supposed to do? It started snowing—it was as bad out as it is now." She pointed at the window.

"So I walked to the house and knocked on the door. I thought I'd find William's family, but a woman answered who I'd never seen before. She took one look at me and drew me in. 'Laura,' she cried, 'I declare! We weren't expecting you for another week. What a little bitty thing you are.' And then she sort of shrieked and said, 'Oh, you poor dear thing, where is your trunk? And your cloak?' Of course, I didn't know what to say, so I just stood there in a kind of daze. The woman's voice sounded strange to me. It was a different accent from the people in Garnet. Her clothes were odd, too. And the house! Somehow it wasn't William's at all, anymore. It had completely different furniture and was painted and wallpapered, and full of all sorts of things on shelves. The woman hustled me over to a warm seat near the fireplace and wrapped me in a shawl. 'Just rest now, dear. It's clear to me you have met with some misadventure, and I'll want to hear all about it. But now you need to get warmed up.' "

Abby pleated the envelope as she spoke. "So I drank her mulled cider and warmed up by the fire, and wondered what on earth had happened to me. I figured I wasn't dead after all—surely heaven wouldn't look like the Prindle House. I must have been in shock, I guess. I couldn't imagine what was going on. But then—" Her voice lowered, and Miranda and Dan had to lean forward to hear her. "Then suddenly I noticed the needlework—it was a sampler—the woman had been working on. It was lying on the chair next to mine, and I straightened it out to see properly." She paused. "That was when I knew something impossible had happened. The date on the sampler was 1756—more than sixty years in the future!"

Miranda had been following Abby's story as if watching a film; she could picture it all so exactly. The bedraggled, frightened girl brought into an unfamiliar house, warming herself in front of a fire, her mind in turmoil. And then seeing the needlework, grabbing it up to check the date—and then what? What do you do when you discover the impossible has happened? How had Abby coped? Miranda gazed at Abby with new respect.

"So what did you do then?" asked Dan eagerly. He no longer seemed afraid of Abby.

"What could I do? When the woman came

back with my drink, I asked her what town we were in, and what colony. I just had to be sure. She said, 'Garnet, of course. In Massachusetts. Dear child, has something happened to addle your wits?' She thought I was Laura, her cousin's daughter from Philadelphia who was coming to stay after having been orphaned. The woman—her name was Matilda Prindle—was good to me. I stayed with her, telling her I had no recollection of what had happened to my trunk, my cloak, or anything. She believed I had been set upon by thieves, and so traumatized that I lost my memory—you know, you call it amnesia now."

Abby pursed her lips thoughtfully. "I let her think what she wanted. At the time, I didn't know what to think about what had happened, either. Maybe I *had* lost my memory. How could I know? Certainly I realized something amazing had happened. You wouldn't believe how frightened I was when I walked around Garnet with Matilda Prindle and saw places I recognized, but all changed. It was like something out of a nightmare. And the people! I saw faces I thought I almost recognized . . . I went to Thomas's house—my brother's—but the house had become a milliner's." She glanced at Miranda's perplexed expression. "A hat shop," she explained. "It was right where The Sassy Café is now."

Abby hugged herself and continued. "I discovered horrible things. That Thomas and Sarah were dead, and their children, Charity, Nicholas, and Daniel, too. Dead from old age! I learned that Charity had married into the Prindle family and that Matilda's husband, Tobias, was her son. Little Charity's son—I couldn't believe it. She was just a baby, practically, when I knew her. Can you imagine how it was for me to believe that somehow—in an instant— the little children I knew had grown up, led their whole lives through, had children and grandchildren—all in the time it took me to whirl through that wind?"

"I'd never have believed any of this if I hadn't seen you disappear," Dan said under his breath.

Abby creased the envelope into a square. "Anyway, I stayed with this new generation of Prindles as long as I could. When Matilda Prindle's cousin Laura showed up at last a week later, I had already made myself helpful to the family. Matilda and Tobias had four children, and they let me stay on with them as a sort of housekeeper or poor relation. I did a lot of the work, but I also got to eat meals with the family and take lessons with their two daughters. Laura, the cousin, was a few years older than me, but we soon became friends. It was hard to leave. . . ." Abby's voice trailed off.

"But why did you leave them at all?" Miranda asked. "Why not just explain what had happened to you, awful and bizarre though it was, and stay?"

"Because memory lasts a long, long time. The people of Garnet—my Garnet, that is—were afraid of witchcraft. We saw it everywhere. It seemed to be all around us, in the air, anyplace. The people in Matilda and Tobias's Garnet thought they had finally put that fear behind them. But after a few years, people couldn't help but notice I wasn't changing. And the whispers of witchcraft started again. I couldn't bear it. Even later, when people didn't believe in witches so readily anymore, I'd have been enough to convince them all over again." Abby threw down the manila envelope and hugged herself again. "I don't grow. Nothing changes at all." She stretched out her hand. "Look, my nails haven't grown since the fire. And my hair hasn't, either." She held out her foot and peeled off the sock. "Look at this. See that bruise?"

Miranda and Dan gazed at the dark blue fleck on the knuckle of Abby's big toe.

"Well, that happened about a week before the fire when I dropped an iron ladle on my toe while I was helping my mother make stew. The bruise hasn't gone away in all this time. Same with the burn on my thigh—it never healed. At first I kept putting ointment on it, and bandages—but then I noticed it never changed at all. It didn't get better, but it didn't get any worse. It hurt—but I learned to live with the pain. I hardly ever notice it now."

"I guess you'd get used to just about anything in three hundred years," said Dan.

Abby pulled her sock back on. "I always have to move on before people notice there's something weird about me. Sooner or later, someone notices I'm still a kid. I never get taller. I never"—she glanced down at her small breasts—"never develop much." Her smile was rueful. "I think the wind threw me into a time warp or something after the fire and kicked me into the future. I just thank God I wasn't ill with smallpox or a fever then, or else I'd still be ill today."

"You mean you never get sick or hurt?" marveled Dan.

"Oh, sure I do. It seems to be only the things that happened to me *before* the fire that never change." Her mouth twisted. "I've had plenty of cuts and bruises in my time, believe me. But they all healed normally—and whenever I got sick, I got better again, even though I sometimes prayed I'd die. But I'm stuck with this burn and this bruise. And this girl's body and brain."

Miranda stood up and prowled restlessly around the bedroom. "And that old man who died? The one you were living with in Baltimore? Who was he really?"

"His name was Louis Horner, and I was sort of acting as his nurse. I like living with old people. I can help them as much as they help me, and they aren't so quick to turn me in to the authorities. But of course when he died, he left the house to his own relatives. I had to get out of there fast before people arrived for the funeral."

"But how do you move on when you have to leave?" Miranda couldn't imagine how it would feel to be on her own, without her parents. She stared out the window. The snow was falling so thickly that she could only barely make out the outlines of her house across the road. "Do you just run off without even leaving a note?"

Abby sighed and fingered a packet of photographs. "Oh, sometimes I leave a letter, sometimes not. I just move on, but it's never easy leaving the people you care about—over and over again. It's wrenching. You never get used to it."

Dan reached for Miranda's hand. "How do you choose where to go next?" he asked.

"I'm drawn back to Garnet, but I have to be careful not to come here more than once every fifty years or so. I can't risk having people recognize me. But Garnet's my real home. I belong here. It was hard, that first time, to leave the Prindles. At least they were related to me—through Charity, you see. I didn't know where to go from there. But I left them a note saying thank you for everything, and just ran away to Boston one night. I found work in a tavern as a serving girl. Once Tobias Prindle was in Boston, visiting his brother. They walked in—and I panicked. I couldn't let Tobias see me. After that, I made sure I moved farther away."

"Tobias Prindle." Dan spoke the name quietly. "Now I remember where I've heard that name before. There's a letter written by a Tobias Prindle—something about witchcraft—in the Prindle House exhibit now. Could it be the same man?"

"Probably," nodded Abby. "I'd like to see that letter. It seems to me Tobias *had* published something in the newspaper—I think I remember people talking about it."

"Well, where did you go when you ran away again?" asked Dan.

"To Concord. I helped on a farm. I stayed there during the war."

"During the war?" Miranda looked perplexed. "What war?"

"The American Revolution," said Abby. "You know."

Miranda's eyes opened wide. "You must be a walking history book! You must know everything there is to know—the real, inside stories about everything. Did you meet Benjamin Franklin and Thomas Jefferson and everybody? All the founding fathers— Just think of it, Dan. Abby was right there."

Abby sighed. "I was there, all right. Milking cows and weeding the vegetable garden, trying to grow enough food to feed the hungry British soldiers that were billeted with the family. But that's as close as I came to fame and glory. Think about it, Mandy. Have you met the president? Do you know the inside story about what's happening in politics?"

Miranda frowned, disappointed.

"Oh, I did a lot of things," continued Abby. "In the early 1800s I worked for rich families in New York and Boston. That's when I was with the Longridges. When I left them, I had to get out of town fast. I went west with a family who had a land grant. I helped with all their children and stayed out in Kansas for a long time. . . ." Her voice faltered. She looked at Miranda and Dan sitting shoulder to shoulder on the bed and sighed. "I fell in love—and got married."

"Married!" cried Dan.

"But you're only thirteen!" objected Miranda.

"I felt a lot older by then." Abby shrugged. "And it was easier then to decide who you wanted to be. There wasn't so much bureaucracy, you know? No tax forms or social security numbers. You were freer, then. It was easy to say I was sixteen—just small for my age. Oh, maybe some people didn't buy the story, but so what? There I was—an orphan. If a homesteader needed a wife, who would object?"

"What happened?" pressed Dan. "Did you just walk out of the marriage?"

"Did you have any children?" asked Miranda.

"No and no," answered Abby. "I didn't have children, thank goodness. And I wasn't married long because Luke—Luke died." She fell silent, and Miranda sensed not to push. No matter that more than a hundred years had passed; this was a sadness still raw.

"It was easier to move around once trains were in use," said Abby. "I could go farther—and faster. I needed to get away from the places I'd lived so no one would recognize me. I went to San Francisco and invented another story, but after the big earthquake in 1906, I came back east. I was homesick for Garnet and had been away a long time." She sighed. "It's so hard. You have no idea. Always moving on . . . leaving people you care about. Always trying not to care too much about anybody because you know it can't last. That's another reason I like old people best. They die—and I don't have to just leave them in the lurch."

"What was it like when you came back to Garnet? Did you stay long?" asked Dan. Miranda imagined the future museum curator in him was regarding Abby as a special exhibit.

"I worked as an assistant teacher. The schoolhouse was the Prindle House, can you imagine? But I didn't stay long. The teacher I was working with moved north, up to a little Maine fishing village, and she took me along with her as her assistant."

"Did you ever get married again?" asked Miranda.

Abby looked sad. "No. By then it was too risky. You had to have licenses—proof of age. I did fall in love one other time—not very long ago at all. It was in the late 1960s, in Philadelphia. The man wanted to be a writer—he said I inspired him, that I was his muse. But I had to leave him, too—and then later I heard he'd died young. But it's always that way. Whether they die young or old, everybody I've ever known has died."

She hesitated, then spoke again. "When I'm feeling sad, which is most of the time, I go back to the ruin of my house. It's easy to do—I just wish myself there, and I'm riding back through that wind, back to the rubble and ash. There I'm like a ghost. Time is exactly as I left it. My brother is searching for me, and I try to tell him I'm there but I can't. And I can't leave the site. I'm stuck there. Time just stands still. So I leave, and I'm back in the real world where time goes on and I'm the only thing that doesn't."

Abby dropped the manila envelope. It was creased and torn. "Finding a family is always the hardest part. It used to be easier, but as time goes on, I can't find people to take me in so readily. Earlier I could find work as a maid in a big house or pose as some lost relation. But now"—she laughed harshly—"people are smarter. They don't fall for that anymore. And the child labor laws make it hard for me, too. And there are no servants—at least not servants who are as little as I am. If I don't watch out now, I'll end up in foster care, or in an orphanage again—like I did in the 1930s. . . ." She shook her head and frowned over at Miranda. "You knew, Mandy. But I couldn't tell you then."

"I knew?" Miranda was confused. Then she understood. "Oh, Abby, then *you* were the girl Nonny remembered! It wasn't your grandmother at all."

"I was back here in Garnet again, camping out in the woods up on the hill. Talk about irony. First the Prindle House was William's family's home—and might have been mine, too, if we'd married. Then it was where I lived with Matilda and Tobias. More than a century later I was teaching school right in the living room—and then only about twenty years after that, when the new schools were built, it became a horrid old orphanage, run like a prison, and I was an inmate—thanks to Susannah's great-granny."

"Well, I bet you didn't stay long," said Dan. "I bet you ran away again."

"Of course I did. I always do. But deciding to leave is difficult. You've seen homeless people. It's *hard* out there on the streets."

Miranda shifted uncomfortably as she remembered following Abby on her search for food through the snowy streets.

Abby selected a faded photo in sepia tone and handed it to Miranda. "Look, here it is. The Prindle Home for Female Children. An official picture of the whole lot of us." She pointed to the front row. "And there's yours truly."

Miranda peered at the photograph, squinting to see the features of the thin figure standing rail-straight, her pale hair pulled back in two long braids. She passed the picture to Dan. "Those braids look too tight," she said in a low voice. What else was there to say?

CHAPTER
THIRTEEN

WHEN MRS. HOOTON called them for pizza,
Dan, Miranda, and Abby trooped downstairs.
"Don't say anything," begged Abby. "Please
don't tell anyone."

They joined Helen, Philip, and Buddy in
the dining room, where two extra-large pizzas
waited on the table. Miranda noticed how
pleased her parents looked at the sight of Miranda and Abby together. Dan's parents entered
from the kitchen carrying a tossed salad and a
tray with drinks. "This isn't like a regular dinner party," Buddy piped up. He was accus-
tomed to the formal entertaining his parents did
when the museum's board of directors came to
dinner. "It's more like family."

"Our extended family." Virginia Hooton
smiled and passed Miranda the salad.

Miranda tried to throw herself into the spirit of the lighthearted gathering, but her mind was occupied with all Abby had told them. She ate her salad and two pieces of mushroom pizza, chewing slowly while she thought. Dan, too, was subdued, though he managed to consume his usual five pieces of pizza. Abby, on the other hand, was more animated than usual. She joked with Buddy while she ate and plied Mr. and Mrs. Hooton with questions about their museum.

"What are the earliest exhibits?" she wanted to know.

"Oh, we have things from the seventeenth century," Ed Hooton told her. "Mostly household items. It's amazing—some of the tools people used daily we don't have a clue about today. Dan and I put together a children's quiz for classes that take the museum tour, and the children have to guess how various tools and utensils were used. It's been very successful and popular with teachers."

"Kids today don't know very much about history," said Abby with a smirk.

Miranda glanced over at her and grinned. Abby's superior tone, usually so grating on Miranda's nerves, seemed well earned after all she had told them earlier. "But you always manage to get A's in *your* history classes, don't you?" Miranda teased.

"Oh," said Virginia Hooton brightly. "Are you especially interested in history, Abby?"

"You could say that." Abby helped herself to another slice of pizza.

Outside, the wind howled, but inside Miranda played cards with Buddy, Abby, and Dan in the kitchen while the parents talked over coffee and cheesecake in the dining room. Miranda found it hard to concentrate on their game. Her mind was whirling with possibilities and impossibilities, and she itched to ask Abby more questions. Finally Helen and Philip thanked the Hootons for having them over and bundled up against the cold to cross the street back to their own house. When they'd reached the porch, Miranda stopped and turned back to Abby. "Let's go for a walk," she said in a low voice.

"But it's snowing. It's practically a blizzard."

"But we need to talk—especially if you think I can help you. I think better when I walk."

Helen unlocked the front door. Philip stepped inside and removed his scarf. "Coming girls?" he asked.

"Not yet," said Miranda. "We're going for a little walk."

"A walk!" exclaimed Helen. "In this weather you'll need skis."

Philip put his hand on her shoulder. "Let them go," he said. They exchanged a hopeful look.

"Well, don't go far," cautioned Helen. "It's dark and already quite late—and you both have school tomorrow."

They promised to return soon and set off. The moon lit the road through the flurries, its glow nearly as bright as day. After walking for nearly five minutes, silent except for the crunch of snow under their boots, Miranda shyly linked her arm through Abby's.

"Nice," Abby said, squeezing Miranda's arm. "Friends always used to walk this way. I miss it."

The simple comparison between "then" and "now" touched Miranda. She realized she no longer doubted Abby's story. Excitement soared in Miranda, submerging the confusion and frustration of the past weeks. But all she said was, "So how do you do it? Travel through time."

"I don't travel around, you know. I told you—I can only go back to that one time and place, to the ruin, just after everyone died."

"Then why go, if you can't do anything?" asked Miranda logically. "If all you can do there is cry, why make yourself miserable? You can't change anything."

Abby slid on a patch of icy sidewalk and clutched Miranda's arm more tightly to regain her balance. "It's like an addiction, I think. I feel this pull. I don't expect you to understand. It's this *urgency*. And so I go back whenever I feel like it—whether I'm at school or home or anywhere, I can just disappear. And when I return, only a short time has passed. Sometimes I hover back at the site of my house for what seems to me like days, but when I let go and return to the present—whenever the present is—it's maybe only an hour later."

"Hmm." Miranda kicked up snow with her boots as they walked. "I wonder how it happened to you in the first place. I mean, what saved you from the fire? What was different about you from the other people who died?"

Abby stopped walking. "I'm *not* a witch, Mandy!"

Miranda looked at her in surprise. "Who said anything about witches? I'm just trying to figure out why you were saved when no one else was. Maybe you have a guardian angel or something. Anyway, you know there's no such thing as witches."

Abby started walking again. She shoved her hands into the pockets of her denim coat. "You may know that, but it's taken me a long time."

"What do you mean?"

Abby's breath hung in white puffs as she explained. "It was such a different time, Mandy. People were different in Garnet when I first lived here—and it was more than just clothing and manners. You have no idea. People believed in devils and witches. Anything we didn't understand could be attributed to witchcraft. You must have studied the Salem witch trials in school."

Miranda nodded. "Yeah, that was when some stupid girls accused a bunch of women of being witches and torturing them and stuff, right? And so the women were sentenced to death."

"Right. But it wasn't just a few women who were sentenced, and it wasn't just in Salem. It happened in Garnet, too. The whole of New England was all worked up about witches when I was a girl. When anything strange happened, people panicked."

"Did you believe in witches? Do you still?"

Abby was silent for a moment. "I guess I did. Now, I don't know what to think. *Something* happened to me, that's for sure. If it wasn't witchcraft, then what was it? There was a woman who lived in the woods—up on the hill behind the cemetery. She was Indian, or part Indian. Her name was Willow. She used to come into town to barter for food. She grew herbs, and she could heal people even when nothing else worked. She saved one of my sisters from a fever once, when others in the village died of it. She was wild and strange and used to mutter things to herself as she walked. People pretty much stayed away from her, but after she saved my sister, they started coming to her when they needed her help. I was a little bit afraid of her, but fascinated, too. I guess I thought she might be a witch. Other people did." She glanced at Miranda beneath snow-tipped lashes. "And for a long time after the fire, I worried I must be a witch, too. How else to explain being shot forward into the future the way I was? I was scared people would notice that I never changed and accuse *me* of witchcraft. Oh, Mandy, they hanged witches. It was a horrible way to die. I can't bear to think about it."

Miranda took her arm again. *For all of Ab-*

by's long years of experience, Miranda thought, *the small, scared Puritan girl Abby had once been still lurked close beneath the surface of the modern girl.* "Well, look, if it wasn't a magic spell that saved you from the fire and threw you into the future, what *was* it?"

"I can't think," said Abby. "Unless it was the charm that Willow gave me." She smiled sadly at Miranda through the flurries of snow that settled like a blanket around them. "But I lost it long ago."

"What charm?" Miranda demanded as they reached the top of the hill and stopped.

Abby fingered a strand of long hair that had escaped from her woolen hat. "It was a small stone carving. My mother sent me to Willow's house in the woods to bring her a chicken as thanks for curing Constance's fever. It was already months after the sickness was gone, but my mother was so grateful, I took things to Willow often. Loaves of bread and fish and wampum—beads made from periwinkle shells, you know, from the coast. Sometimes she let me stay while she worked in her garden. We never talked, but I loved the smell of the herbs and flowers. It was always so peaceful there. Anyway, the day I brought her the chicken, she took the crate and set it down by a tree, and then placed her hands on my head, not saying anything. I was afraid to move or speak. After a while she reached into her skirt and brought out a little statue.

"Willow held it out to me and smiled. When I didn't take it, she pointed to the chicken, which was clucking and scratching in its box, and said, 'A bird for a bird.' So I took it. She said, 'This carving is older than time. It is for second chances.' I was scared—she really *did* seem like a witch, Mandy—so I dropped the carving into my apron pocket and ran back to my house. I never even said thank you." Abby shrugged her shoulders and dislodged a shower of powdery flakes. "I never saw her again. But even though I knew my parents would forbid me to keep it, I carried the little statue with me all the time. Later, when the house burned down, I had it in my apron pocket. It was the only thing I had with me besides the clothes I was wearing when I left my own time."

"So how did you lose it?" Miranda asked.

They had trudged through the snow up one side of the long street and now crossed over to walk down the other side. They leaned against each other when the wind blew to ward off the chill.

"It was stolen, actually." Abby frowned.

"I was living in Boston then—it was 1853 or 1854. I was a housemaid for the Longridge family. They were a good family to work for, but my time there ended in total disaster." She sighed, remembering. "They were rich as anything; Captain Longridge imported all sorts of things from around the world. He was always setting out on voyages and coming back with treasures that they'd put on display."

"What happened?"

"Well, Captain Longridge collected everything—jewelry, paintings, china, silver, you name it. But he was especially interested in statues. He had some Greek and Roman pieces, and other things, too. Little medallions and stone carvings from Africa and Asia. He told me some of the carvings were thousands of years old. He kept them in a glass cupboard, and I dusted them once a month. One day he came home while I was cleaning his study. I hurried to leave—one of the rules of the house was that the servants were never to be seen by the family. But Captain Longridge started talking to me about his collection of statues as I dusted them, and so of course I listened. I was just trying to make polite conversation when I told him about my own little carving. He asked to see it, so I went up to my room in the attic where I kept it hidden under my mattress. When I brought it down, he went crazy. He said he absolutely had to have it for his collection, that it was very old and valuable, and that he'd give me a lot of money for it. Enough so I wouldn't have to work as a maid anymore."

Miranda felt a little thrill of excitement flicker through her body. But she kept her voice even as she hugged Abby's arm and asked: "You didn't sell it to him, though, did you?"

"No . . ." Abby shook her head. "I couldn't. You see, it was the only thing I had that came from my own time. I couldn't let it go."

"I can understand that." Again excitement seized Miranda. "But the money would have helped you—"

Abby's voice rang out in the dark angrily. "That's what he kept saying! The money, the money, the money—he seemed to think that's all I needed to be happy. He grabbed for the statue and said he would have it, no matter what—and I ran. I ran to my room and he followed me. There was no way to get out of the attic, so I did the only thing I could to escape—I wished myself back to my own time. And there I was at the ruin, miserable as ever, but safe."

"And you never went back again? To the Longridges', I mean?"

"I stayed at the ruin as long as I could bear it, longer than ever before. But even though it's hard to stay away, it's also horrible being there. So eventually I let myself return to the present—and when I appeared back at the Longridges' hardly any time had passed at all. My room was full of people. Everyone screamed and ran when they saw me." She laughed hollowly. "You see, I hadn't been careful. Captain Longridge saw me vanish. He was frightened out of his skull and summoned the police, the preacher, the whole family. And he told them I'd tried to steal one of his statues. All those people were waiting there to see what would happen—and then I reappeared.

" 'Seize her!' someone shouted, and the constables rushed toward me. Captain Longridge grabbed my little statue and the police carried me away." She let out a long breath. "They put me in the police wagon. But of course I disappeared back to Garnet as soon as I could, and stayed there even longer, waiting at the ruin until I figured enough time had passed so I could go back. When I returned to the present, a few hours had passed. The police cart was parked outside the courthouse. No one

was around—they were probably all out looking for me—so I was able to slip away. Of
course, I had to leave Boston."

"Did you find a new family to live with?"
asked Miranda, her voice full of concern.

Abby squeezed her arm. "Oh, of course. I
always do. I went to New York, where I took
a position as a companion to Deborah Peterson.
And when I left them, I went west. That's
how I met Luke on the wagon trail to Kansas.
Oh—it was all a long time ago. Marrying him,
watching him sicken. . . ." Her voice trailed
off. Snow crunched under their boots as they
made their way back to the house. Fine powdery snow sifted off Abby's hat, nearly the
color of her hair. "Anyway, I managed to survive. Somehow I keep on managing."

Miranda stuffed her hands deep into her
pockets as they turned into her driveway. Despite the welcome lights from the living room
windows, she felt lost. Abby was so old. So
incredibly, impossibly old. She might still have
a thirteen-year-old's body, and a thirteen-year-
old's emotions, but the long years of living must
have given her the wisdom and experience of a
much older soul. Miranda longed suddenly for
the snide, smirky Abby. *She* could be dealt
with. But a mystical, long-suffering Abby was

something else again. The girl at her side had known one loss after another, more losses than Miranda could imagine. Her husband, her family, her friends, her possessions—everything she treasured—time had stolen them all away.

But maybe not everything, after all.

"So you never got your statue back?" Miranda asked casually as they climbed the porch steps.

"Nope," said Abby sadly. "Never saw that old phoenix again."

And Miranda smiled.

CHAPTER FOURTEEN

MIRANDA GRABBED Abby's hand and pulled her to a stop. "I have to tell you before I burst," she said. "I have a statue of a phoenix, too. I bought it from Dan at the flea market. Mrs. Hooton said it had been donated to the museum in a box with a lot of things from Boston."

Abby stared at her, then opened the door and stepped inside. "A lot of people might have statues of birds." She shrugged off her heavy coat and hung it in the closet. "Mine was unique. It was a whistle."

"Mine is a whistle, too!" Miranda tossed her coat into the closet and tugged Abby toward the stairs. "Come on upstairs where we can be private, and I'll show you."

Miranda crossed straight to her window seat and sank down, digging into the pocket of her jeans. "Here it is," she said, and held the little figure to her lips. As she blew the sweet note into the air, Abby's eyes grew wide. Silently she reached out her hand, and Miranda placed the phoenix in her palm.

Abby turned the phoenix over and over in her hands, her eyes closed. She pressed the cold stone to her face, against one cheek, then put it to her lips and blew.

"Well?" Miranda was eager, deeply expectant.

Abby lifted tear-filled eyes to Miranda's. "Oh, Mandy," she whispered. "It *is* my phoenix." She picked at the green felt that covered the bottom as a protective base. "But this shouldn't be here. It's covering up the little woman."

"What woman?"

Abby handed the statue back to Miranda. "Go on, take it off and we'll see. My hands are shaking too much."

Miranda scraped at the circle of felt with her fingernail.

"Peel it off," urged Abby. "Captain Longridge probably stuck it on so the statue wouldn't scratch his precious display tables. But when Willow gave me the bird, it was pure stone. Can you see it yet? On the base there should be a picture of a woman with a basket or something balanced on her head. It's hard to see, it's so small." Abby waited impatiently until Miranda pulled the last of the old felt from the base of the whistle.

The tiny etching was primitive, scratched deep into the stone. A female figure, arms raised to hold the urn or basket she carried on her head, faced sideways, one foot lifted slightly as if she were in motion. Miranda and Abby bumped heads as they bent over the phoenix. Miranda let out her breath in a ragged gasp.

"Oh, Abby!" She sank back, grinning. "It *is* yours. I knew it had to be."

Abby stared at her with round eyes. "But how?"

"Because there has to be a link between us. Why do you think I'm supposed to help you? Why can I hear your crying when no one else ever has before? Why me? It isn't as if we're close or share any special bond. . . . I mean we're both about the same age, both girls, we go to the same school and so on, but that's the sort of thing you've had in common with lots of people. I didn't know what else there could be until you told me the story tonight. Abby, listen. You've never lived with someone before who had your phoenix!"

Abby cradled the statue to her. "Old bird," she murmured with a faraway smile. "What a trip it has been for you! All the way from the Indian woman to my pocket, then to Captain Longridge's collection, then to the Garnet High School flea market. . . ."

"And into my pocket." Miranda laughed. "And only God knows where else before."

They were silent, each thinking about the long journey the phoenix had made to be re- united with Abby here in this room. After a while Abby spoke. "So now we have proof that you're meant to help me. But *how?* That's what we've got to figure out."

Miranda frowned. "I wonder if the phoenix is the key. I mean, you had it in your apron pocket when the fire started, right? It's some- thing you had that no one else did. I bet it is what saved you. Remember what Willow said about second chances? And I felt weird when- ever I blew it. In fact, I had it with me each time I heard you crying. So the phonenix must have *let* me hear you. It must have some ancient, powerful magic."

Abby was paler than ever. "I told you, peo- ple in the village thought Willow was a witch."

"I don't believe in witches, Abby."

"But you said you think the phoenix is

magic. How can you believe in magic and not believe in witches?"

Miranda bit her lip. "I don't know. But I guess I just believe in powers beyond what we can understand. It's like with religion. We don't understand everything, but we see evidence of God all around. Maybe some people understand things better than others—maybe the Indian woman was that kind of person. That doesn't mean she was a witch."

Abby regarded her silently, clutching the phoenix tightly in her lap.

"But what an amazing gift," Miranda continued. "It saved your life. It's fantastic." *And now it's mine*, she thought with a sudden leap of her heart. Did that mean she, too, would be safe from death now? She reached out her hand for the phoenix and, slowly, Abby gave it to her. As her fingers closed on the cold stone, Miranda felt relief surge through her body. "Safe forever," she murmured.

Abby shook her head. "Safe from death, yes. But that isn't everything, believe me."

"Just think of it, Abby," said Miranda dreamily. "If our house caught on fire right now—or if the school bus got into a crash, or whatever—then maybe *I'd* be the one catapulted into the future. I'd be just like you,

Abby. Do you think I'd be drawn back to this time, to the ruin of my house, just like you're drawn back to the ruin of yours?" It was a fantastic notion. Then another idea gripped her. "Hey, maybe that's what happened to Willow herself! Maybe that's how she got the phoenix in the first place."

"You mean someone gave it to her once, and it saved her from death, and she lived nearly forever? You mean, when she gave me the statue, she might have been hundreds of years old already—and no one ever knew?"

"It would be easier to hide the fact that you never changed if you were already grown up when you were saved by the phoenix," Miranda decided. She stroked it, marveling at her good fortune. "I'll have to make sure I always carry you with me, little bird."

"But—but the phoenix isn't yours," said Abby. "It's mine."

Miranda stared at her. "Don't be selfish. You've already had your big rescue."

Abby shook her head. "Willow gave it to me. No one gave it to you."

"Yeah, but I bought it. It was a legal transaction."

"No, it was dealing in stolen goods. Believe me, I've lived long enough to know all about the law. Mandy, I think the phoenix came to you specially so that we would be linked. So that you can help me return to my family."

Miranda, fingers closed tightly around the phoenix, resisted Abby's words. One part of her couldn't bear to give up the phoenix now that she knew what it could do. It would be like throwing away a life raft that drifted her way after a shipwreck.

But I haven't been in a shipwreck, another part of her argued. *I have everything, and Abby has nothing.*

Would the magic still work if the phoenix were not given freely? Had its magic worked for Captain Longridge, who had stolen it from Abby? Did the fact that the phoenix had ended its circuitous journey in Miranda's possession mean she had been specially chosen to help Abby? The answers to these questions drifting through Miranda's mind seemed important, but she felt too confused to figure out why. She looked over at Abby's tight, miserable face.

"I don't see why you need me at all," Miranda said. "Can't you just wish yourself back into the past *before* the fire the same way you wish yourself to the ruin? You could go back and cancel the birthday celebration for William. Make sure you're out of the house on the day the roof catches. Or, better yet, don't light a fire at all that day. Climb up on the roof and pour buckets of water all over to wet it, just to make sure. Then there wouldn't be a fire, and your family wouldn't get killed. You'll be with them, and you'll have done it on your own, and you won't have needed the phoenix after all." Miranda smiled with satisfaction at having solved Abby's troubles so neatly *and* found a way to keep the phoenix for herself.

"I'm not a witch, Mandy! I can't just wish myself to whatever time I want. Believe me, I've tried and tried. You don't understand. Whenever I go back, I find myself trapped at the ruin." She shook her head. "The phoenix has linked us up, and I think that's important. It must mean you can use its power." She brightened. "Maybe that's why it found you. Maybe it will let *you* wish yourself back in time and save us all before the fire starts."

"Me?" Miranda laughed uncomfortably.

"Won't you please try?" begged Abby. "Go back and stop the fire from starting? Think of how you feel about Dan. What if something happened so you never saw him again—until you met me and learned I might have the power to help you. Wouldn't you want me to try everything possible?"

Miranda lay back on the window seat and closed her eyes. She thought about Dan. What if she were snatched away from him now—and lived on for hundreds of years without him? "Oh, all right. All right, already," she relented. "I'll wish myself back there right now." Resolved, Miranda stood up and took the phoenix from Abby. "What do I do? Just close my eyes and wish—wish what?"

"Wait!" Abby jumped up, too. "You mustn't—I mean, you have to be careful."

Exasperated, Miranda looked at Abby.

"Maybe we both should go, Mandy," mused Abby. "I mean, I know I don't have the power to go back further than the fire myself, but if you do, and if you hold hands with me, maybe we'll *both* be transported."

Miranda tugged her fingers nervously through her curls. "I never thought about what I'll do if it really works," she admitted. "What if people can see me, and they all think I'm a witch?" Talking about time travel was fine when *Abby* was the time traveler. But Miranda felt she was looking into a void when she attempted to picture herself in a time long before she was born. Her head began to ache dully. She laughed uncertainly.

"Oh, please," urged Abby. "We just need to take some precautions."

"Precautions?"

Abby frowned. "We'll need clothes. And—I know! We'll take Dan along, too. That way, the two of you will be together if anything—happens."

"Abby! What do you mean?"

"I just wouldn't want you to be without him the way I've been without William."

Miranda rubbed her eyes. She felt as if she might wake up any moment and find this whole conversation with Abby had been a dream. Maybe the past several weeks were all just part of a weird dream. It was a comforting thought.

Then Abby touched her on the arm. "The phoenix."

With a groan, Miranda handed it to her. Maybe the phoenix was all just part of the dream, too.

"Good." Abby stowed the phoenix in her pocket. "Now you go call Dan and tell him what's happening. Tell him to come over here—or we'll go there, if he wants. I'll write the letter."

"What letter?" Things were going too fast for Miranda. She felt dazed.

"If we just disappear without saying anything, your parents might worry about you. It's going to be hard enough for you to explain where I am when I don't come back with you."

Miranda hadn't considered that angle at all. "Wait a minute. They'll be really upset. They'll have the police looking for you, and the child welfare people. They'll think you were kidnapped or something. And they'll stick me in an asylum when I try to explain."

"That's why I'm going to write the letter. Oh, Mandy, don't chicken out on me now."

"I'm not . . ."

"Good." Abby sighed with relief. "So I'll write it now while you arrange things with Dan. I'll tell them I've gone to a distant fourth cousin I just remembered I had. In—in Canada, someplace. And, wait a sec—you'd better find something to wear. At least wear a long skirt. Otherwise, if the phoenix really does give you the power to take us back before the fire, and if people can see us, you'll be locked in the stocks for indecency."

Miranda's eyes widened. "I don't know what I have. What will you take?"

"Oh, just an old thing I've saved." She went to Miranda's desk, sat down, and reached for pen and paper.

Miranda walked slowly to her parents' bedroom to phone Dan. He was silent when she outlined their plan.

After a long moment he finally spoke. "You don't really think this will work, do you?"

"Dan—I just don't know. But you said yourself we had to try to help Abby. She's certain I'm meant to go back and fix things so that her house doesn't burn." She kept her voice low. "She thinks the phoenix will give me the power to travel back. If it doesn't work, what have we got to lose? And if it does work—oh, Dan. I need you to be with me."

She listened to the silence, clutching the receiver. Finally he answered. "You're on."

They arranged to meet back at his house in fifteen minutes. Miranda told him to find an old-time costume. Then she hung up and ran to her room to hunt for something that would pass as a long Puritan skirt. Abby was no longer at the desk.

With a flash of inspiration, Miranda hauled down a big dress box from the top shelf of her closet. Opening it, she pulled out a black, floor-length skirt she had worn as part of a witch costume at the high school's Halloween party. That, a white blouse, and a heavy shawl—borrowed from her mother's closet—would have to suffice. She glanced down at her shoes, deciding that sneakers would not pass muster. So she donned her black snow boots and felt glad that the long skirt hid all but the toes. She looked nothing like a Puritan, but at least no one could say she wasn't decently covered.

Abby met her in the hallway, still dressed in jeans, and handed Miranda a neatly folded piece of paper. "Here's the letter. Better keep it in your desk till you need to give it to your parents." She tried to suppress a smirk at Miranda's costume but failed. Still, her voice was serious. "If people ask what's wrong with your hair, tell them you had scarlet fever and it all fell out. That's why it's so short. And don't you think you should save your costume until we get to Dan's?"

Miranda pulled the costume off rapidly, revealing her own jeans and a sweater. Then she tucked the letter into her top desk drawer and hurried downstairs behind Abby.

Helen and Philip were reading in the living room. The girls stopped in the doorway. "We have to go back to Dan's," Miranda told them. "Just for—for a little while." She hoped that would be true.

"We left something over there," added Abby. She looked at their faces carefully, then sighed. "You know," she said softly, "I have really enjoyed my time with you. Thank you."

They looked back at her curiously. "We're glad," said Philip.

"Hurry back," added Helen. She looked back down at her book.

"We will." Miranda headed for the front door. *If all goes well.*

Outside, Miranda looked up at the icicle daggers hanging from the gutter on the porch roof. Snow had blown onto the porch, dusting the green glider swing with white. Moonlight gleamed on the fresh snow and caught the sparkle of ice in the trees. The girls walked with giant steps across the snow-packed road. Miranda's costume was packed tightly into her bulging bookbag. Abby carried her beaded satchel. Dan was waiting for them just inside the door and held a finger to his lips.

"Ssh, come with me," he whispered, and motioned them down a corridor toward the museum wing of the old house. "I don't want Buddy to hear us. He's just gone to bed, but he'll be out in a second if he hears you. My parents are watching the news. The museum wing is the best place to try this experiment." He winked at Miranda. "If nothing happens, we can sit around in our costumes and feel at home among all the antiques."

How could he joke when Miranda felt so nervous? She followed him and Abby down the hall to the museum wing and entered a small, low-ceilinged room lined with glass-topped display cases. Abby dropped her beaded satchel and began pulling garments out hastily. She turned her back on Dan and Miranda and took off her sweater.

"Let's hurry," she said, her voice muffled as she pulled a long dress over her head. "Mandy? Can you help with these buttons?"

Dan stared. "Hey, that dress looks like it could be in one of our exhibits."

Abby held her long hair out of the way so Miranda had access to the row of tiny buttons down the back. "It's from when I worked as a parlor maid for a family named Kauffman in Philadelphia for about three years."

"When?"

"Oh, hmmm." Abby draped a white shawl across her shoulders, her forehead screwed up in thought. "Around 1830 or so. 1836? I forget."

"Give me a break," Dan muttered. As he stood there staring at Abby, Miranda saw something like fear settle into his eyes. Silent, he dressed quickly in knee breeches and a ruffled white shirt.

Miranda whistled. "Pretty fancy."

"Thank my mom for these," he said, his voice shaky. "I got them out of a box she's donating to the Garnet Little Theater."

"The wrong century," said Abby. "Men

didn't wear ruffles in Garnet when I lived here. Don't you have a long cloak or something so that you can cover yourself?"

Dan shook his head, his expression dour. "It seems to me that one old outfit looks pretty much like any other," he muttered.

"And you want to be a museum curator?" sniffed Abby. "Don't be ridiculous. Fashions change every year. Does what we wear now look like what your parents or grandparents wore when they were your age? And there you're only talking about fifty or sixty years."

Miranda noticed Abby didn't say "our age." In fact, Abby seemed more different than ever as they readied themselves for possible adventure. The air of superiority that annoyed Miranda so much now seemed to come from true authority. "Let's get on with this," Miranda said. "If Dan and I look out of place, well, even you will look out of place, Abby, in that dress from 1830 or whenever. Let's just try the experiment. If we need other clothes while we're there, well, we can buy some, I guess. I'm bringing my wallet."

"Buy some with what?" asked Dan. "We couldn't use modern money."

"There aren't any stores anyway," said Abby in exasperation. "Do you think we'll just waltz into a mall and choose new clothes from the racks?" She rolled her eyes. This was the prickly Abby that Miranda knew so well. Miranda looked at Dan, and both of them shrugged.

Abby shook her head at them. "You two. I'd like to see how you'd adapt. I bet the first time you had to do anything—even something simple, like lighting a fire—you'd be crying all over the place."

"What do you mean?" Dan sounded indignant. "I was a boy scout, once."

"No matches, probably," Miranda reminded him.

"Oh. Well—"

"No matches, no light bulbs, no indoor plumbing," said Abby in a singsong. "No TV or radio or film. No airplanes, no computers, no hospitals, no Christmas trees."

"No partridge in a pear tree?" asked Dan.

"Well, maybe wild partridges. But no imported pears!"

"And no bathrooms," added Miranda. "Right?"

"No toilet paper, either." Abby smiled wickedly. "Nothing that you two take for granted. But no bombs, either. No missiles. No air pollution. No crack dealers." She shook her head at them. "It's the same world, but a totally different one, too. And I think you'd have a hard time."

"Come on, Abby, give us a little credit," Dan said lightly. "I almost expect to hear you say, 'Kids nowadays, I declare! What is the world coming to?'" He raised his voice to a falsetto. "Just like my grandmother."

"Just remember, Dan Hooton, that I'm old enough to be your great-great-grandmother's great-great-grandmother."

"So show some respect, you whippersnapper," added Miranda.

Their banter had driven the fearful look from Dan's eyes. He spoke with new confidence. "Look, are we going to try this, or what?"

Abby clasped her hands in front of her. "Yes," she whispered, and Miranda realized that Abby's edginess came from nerves. "Come here. Stand here with me." Abby indicated a place in the center of the room. "Mandy, you hold the phoenix. We'll touch it and touch you at the same time. Just for good measure." She handed Miranda the stone bird.

Dan and Abby each placed a finger on the stone figure Miranda held, then put an arm around her. Miranda edged closer to Dan so that their bodies touched.

"Okay, close your eyes," said Abby.

"Now it's up to you, Mandy, to wish us back—back before the fire. If I'm right about you, the phoenix ought to give you the power. Just remember, you have to wish hard. Think of it as a matter of life or death—*my* life or death. You need to wish for this more than you've ever wanted anything. And then it will work. It *must*."

If wishes were horses, then beggars would ride! Unbidden the words to the old nursery rhyme rose to Miranda's lips, but she bit them back.

"Hang on to your hats," said Dan, and Miranda laughed weakly. She closed her eyes, but she was worried. She wanted to help Abby, she really did. But would the strength of her wanting it be enough to make the phoenix carry them back to a time before the fire at Abby's house? Was that how the magic worked?

They waited a long time, it seemed, but nothing happened. Miranda opened one eye. She found Dan looking at her. They both looked at Abby, whose face was screwed up in concentration. But nothing happened.

Miranda leaned against Dan and relaxed. It was a relief, in a way, that time travel wasn't so easy.

Dan smiled down at her.

Abby's eyes flew open. "You're not trying! Neither of you."

"Oh, Abby, I was," Miranda assured her. "But you see for yourself nothing has changed."

"I really should have packed my contact solution," added Dan, grinning with relief that nothing had happened. "In fact, there are a lot of things I wouldn't want to be caught without. Like what about medicine? What if we got sick?"

"Well, at least we've had our vaccinations," said Miranda. "But I'd miss the daily luxuries. You know, like hot showers and conditioner and toothpaste!" *And deodorant,* she thought. *And tampons.*

"Come on, shut up," snapped Abby.

"All right." Dan sighed. He winked at Miranda as they moved close together again and touched the phoenix with their fingers. "Nice knowing you."

"Ssshh!" hissed Abby. And Dan fell abruptly silent.

The three made a tight knot in that small room, the phoenix at their center. The room was very still. "Close your eyes again," whispered Abby. "This time *I'm* going to wish us back. I'll wish to go back before the fire by one day. And I'm wishing we can be seen, that we will be real to other people." She moved even closer to them. "Wish it harder. Wish it with all your souls."

From somewhere a wind began to blow.

Dan gripped Miranda's hand hard. She kept her eyes closed and squeezed back, trying to concentrate on Pilgrims. When nothing more seemed to happen, she let her mind drift on the currents of wind. Don't think, not of the Puritans, not of Indians, not of witches. *Don't think, don't think, don't think.* The refrain ran through her mind, and she realized it was right; imagining what she had learned from textbooks and television, from modern imagination, could only be false, and would only hold them back from wherever the phoenix might take them.

The wind swirled faster. For a moment fear surged in Miranda's mind, but still she did not open her eyes. She fought her fear back, buried it deep, and imagined herself riding on the currents. Only air, cold, empty air, a biting wind such as she and Abby had felt last night on their walk, then cool air, air that warmed slightly until it seemed to be a fresh breeze with a hint of sea and a taste of salt. Miranda tilted her head back, eyes tightly closed, body pressed against Abby's and Dan's, finger fast on the stone phoenix. The fresh breeze in her head changed suddenly, became heavy, hot, and acrid. Dan coughed. Miranda's eyes stung. And very far away the sound of Abby's voice came to them: "Open your eyes now. We're here."

CHAPTER
FIFTEEN

MIRANDA KNEW she was standing on soft grass instead of floorboards, but at first she could not bring herself to open her eyes. She gasped as the acrid air penetrated her lungs. Her eyes opened on a desolate scene. It was daylight now, and she, Dan, and Abby were standing in a glade about twenty feet from a pile of still-smoking rubble. The hot summer air was heavy with charred bits of wood, cloth, and paper. There was dead silence; even the birds seemed to have deserted the scene. Thick forest surrounded the clearing, except to their right, where a wide path sloped down through dense undergrowth to a large house. Miranda recognized it with a catch of breath: the Prindle House. She was terribly afraid.

Abby's sobs filled the charred air, but for the moment Miranda was helpless to comfort her. Her mind reeled with the sights and sounds and smells of this new place. For a second she felt she couldn't breathe. Then she felt Dan beside her and pressed against him. He gripped her arms so tightly it hurt.

"It *worked*," he whispered raggedly. "Oh, Mandy."

Abby's sobs, painful and wracking, rose to a wail. Miranda stepped closer to her. "Abby?" she whispered.

"It didn't work," she gasped. "We're back at the ruin, and it's just like always. The fire's already happened and there's nothing left to do. Nothing!"

"Oh, Abby," said Dan, and he put his arm around her, drawing her close.

The three of them stood in a huddle, Miranda and Dan staring at each other over Abby's bowed head. Miranda saw in Dan's face the shock she knew must be mirrored in her own. The impossibility of what had just happened to them, the strangeness of this desolate place, left Miranda weak and frightened. She wanted nothing in the world more than to be home with her parents in her own house in her own time. Dan's stricken face was white as he gazed around them. Miranda groped for his free hand and squeezed it hard.

"I want to go home," he whispered.

"Oh, Dan. Me, too."

Abby heard them and, gulping back tears, raised her head. "Oh, Mandy. I was counting on you."

"I'm sorry. I wished as hard as I could."

Abby looked around at the burned ruin, then down at the phoenix in her hand. She threw the statue onto the ground. "But it didn't work."

"Well, *something* worked," said Dan. He stared in wonder at the expanse of wild forest and the wreckage of the house still smoking in front of them. "We're here, all of us."

"Look at the Prindle House," breathed Miranda. "It's amazing. I can't believe it."

"Watch out," hissed Dan. "Here comes someone!"

"Let's hide!" rasped Miranda, fear stabbing sharply as she saw the heavyset man walking toward them from around the side of the Prindle House. He wore a rumpled white shirt and dark pants that buckled just below his knees, and his pale hair was the color of Abby's.

Abby's sad voice stopped her. "It's just Thomas, my brother. But he can't see you. At least he can never see *me*."

Nonetheless, Miranda cowered behind Dan as the man drew nearer. Her fear was in part the dawning realization that this was a real man—not an actor on a stage or in a film or video. This was a real person—from Abby's time. *From the past*. Miranda tried to take it all in as the man continued walking toward them along the path from the Prindle House. This was a person whose thoughts were untroubled by any single thing in the Brownes' morning newspaper. His world was such a different place from the one Miranda knew, there was almost no comparison. He knew nothing of electricity, of nuclear power, of computer technology. His consciousness was untroubled by such every-day things as trains, airplanes, or cars. Forget rockets and space stations. There wasn't even a United States of America yet. The Revolution-ary War was still nearly a century in the future, and the Colony of Massachusetts belonged to England. It was an older, and in many ways, simpler time. Yet despite the man's innocence of Miranda's world, he looked troubled as he stopped at the ruin and passed a hand across his face.

"It's always like this." Abby stamped her foot and sank down to sit on a rock.

"But maybe it's different with the phoe-nix," said Miranda, retrieving the stone whistle from the ground and thrusting it into her hand.

"Take this, and now try to talk to him. See if he can see you when you've got the phoenix."

Abby took the phoenix and stepped forward. "Thomas?" she called to the man, and Miranda caught her breath for a second as he paused. But he wasn't looking at them, merely staring into the ruins of the house. Slowly he started walking through the rubble, bending down every so often to pick up some charred remnant of his family's household.

"I'm nothing here," Abby said bitterly. Her sobs began afresh. "Oh, God, please help me. I hate living like this. I should have died in the fire, too."

"Don't say that," cried Miranda, eyes fixed on Thomas.

"It's true. At least that way I'd be with my family and William. It isn't *fair!*"

The man continued to peer into the rubble. Two other men emerged from the trees behind the Prindle House and started along the path to the ruin. They called out Abby's name.

"She must be here," Thomas called back. "But I can't see where—"

"She couldn't have just disappeared." The two men climbed over a charred beam and stood at his side. The younger one spoke firmly. "It's impossible. All the other bodies have been found and are being prepared."

The language sounded strange to Miranda's ears. It was English, yet spoken with an accent she had not heard before.

"Oh, Thomas," said the older man, who was quite stout, "we all grieve. Do not forget you are not alone in your loss. My own son, my William—" He could not go on.

"Not knowing is unbearable," muttered Thomas, kicking at some blackened stones, once part of the chimney. "Perhaps she escaped unharmed? Could that be it?"

"Oh, Thomas," said the stout man. "Possible, perhaps. But in that case, where is she? Abigail was not a girl to run away. She would have come to you."

"Aye," he muttered thickly, gazing at the ground. Then he raised his head and seemed to look right at the three time travelers. "But if her mind had been addled by the disaster? If she had been hurt and wandered away. . . ." He wheeled around to stare at the forest behind the ruin. "She could be in there. Lost—and afraid."

"We will continue searching, Thomas. The whole village is helping. But we must accept the Lord's will."

"Aye," he grunted, turning over a blackened timber with his boot. "The Lord's will— or something else entirely." When the younger men looked at him questioningly, he turned away. "Come, let's leave this place and help the search parties. There is only sorrow here, and nothing else."

The three men turned together and moved quickly down the lane, away from Miranda, Dan, and Abby. Abby called to them, "But I'm here, Thomas! If only you would see!" She started sobbing again as they started down the rutted road, tried to run after them, but was knocked back onto the grass by a whoosh of wind. She stood up, stunned.

"Abby, are you all right?" Dan helped her stand up again. "What was it?"

"Here—you can feel it, too. It's like a wall of wind—you can't feel it until you try to leave the site of this house." Abby rubbed her eyes. "It's what traps me here."

Dan looped an arm around Abby's shoulders. "You're the Abigail they're looking for, right? It's horrible. Is this what happens every time you come back here?"

Abby sank onto the hillock and nodded. She turned her back. "All these buttons, Mandy. Undo them, please. We're ghosts here. Invisible. And it's too hot for all these layers." Under the long, dark wool dress, Abby still wore her jeans and turtleneck.

Miranda wrenched her gaze away from the small figures of the three men down the road, and unbuttoned Abby's dress. Then she slipped off her own long skirt. Dan rolled up the sleeves of his ruffled shirt and unbuttoned the collar. Miranda bundled all their extra clothes into her mother's shawl and tucked them against a rock.

"But now what?" asked Dan. "It doesn't look like the phoenix has the power to send you farther back in time to save your family. We're stuck here."

"Don't say that, Dan!" Miranda shivered despite the warmth of the summer day. "We're not stuck if Abby wishes us home again. Abby?"

Abby sat motionless, staring stonily at the retreating figures of her brother and neighbors. "I was sure you would help me, Mandy. I really thought you would."

"Come on, Abby. It isn't my fault that the phoenix's magic is hard to figure out."

"If only I could go after them. Even if I can't fix things so the fire never happened, I wish I could tell Thomas I'm safe. It isn't right that he should have to be so miserable, searching for me. Oh, if only I could get through this horrible wind! What good is the phoenix if it can't get me home again?" Impassioned, she drew back her arm and hurled the little statue straight into the barrier of wind.

"Abby!" yelled Dan, and Miranda gasped.

The phoenix passed straight through and bounced on the road. It lay in the dust. "How come it can go through the wind?" demanded Miranda.

"Because it's not a ghost, I guess." Abby folded her arms across her chest. "Lucky bird."

Tentatively, Miranda put her hand out toward the barrier of wind. Powerful currents of warm air swirled against her arm. But she pushed against them, then walked forward. She kept walking, though the wind whipped at her hair and clothes and sucked her breath right out of her lungs, until she was standing by an uncharred grove of pine trees on the far side of the dirt road.

"Mandy!" Abby cried. "How can you do that? How can you just walk through it?"

"I don't know," Miranda called back. "I guess it's because I'm not a ghost, either." She bent down and scooped up the phoenix, then looked down the road at the retreating backs of Thomas and the other men. "Hello!" she called. "Thomas? Can you hear me? Can you see me?" The men did not turn.

Dan pressed through the warm wind to join

her. It tossed his hair and clothes but did not stop him. Reaching Miranda, he wrapped her tightly in his arms, and they both looked back across the road at Abby, who stood, staring at them with longing.

"Go after them," she pleaded. "Run after Thomas. If I can't go, you'll have to be my eyes and ears. Find out how his family's doing. Even if no one can see you, you can try to make them sense your presence."

Miranda turned to Dan. "Should we?"

He looked worried. "I don't know."

"The two men with Thomas are Nathaniel Prindle and Richard Mather," Abby called. "Mr. Prindle is the fat one. He's William's father. Richard was William's friend. They're both good men. Oh, it breaks my heart to be so near, to have them searching for me, and no matter how loudly I scream or yell, no matter what I do, they don't notice me."

"We want to help, but we're afraid. I wish you could come with us," Miranda called to Abby. She would feel so much safer if Abby were with them, she realized.

"You don't wish it half as much as I do."

"But where are we supposed to go?" demanded Dan.

"To Thomas's house," Abby called back.

"He's married to Sarah, and they live in the center of the village. Where The Sassy Café is— in your time. He's a wheelwright, just like my father. I mean, like my father was. They have a daughter, Charity, who is three, and two sons named Nicholas and Daniel—Daniel, just like you, Dan. The boys are four and five."

Miranda wondered what a wheelwright did.

"But what can we do there?" objected Dan. "No one can see us, so what's the point? I think we ought to go home." He scowled.

"I'm afraid, too," whispered Miranda. She stowed the phoenix in her jeans pocket and took Dan's arm. "But we came to try to help Abby, so I think we should go. She hasn't seen her brother's family for years."

"Then let's hurry. I don't like this."

Abby stood, a forlorn figure, watching them from the charred ruin of her house.

Miranda had to force down the panic that throbbed in her stomach as she and Dan tried to walk along the road. Instead of moving normally, their feet seemed to be treading air, as if they were in water. Miranda couldn't quite get a purchase on the ground but drifted just above it. At the ruin she had walked on firm ground, but here, beyond the strange wall of wind, the law of gravity did not seem to apply.

"We're like—like ghosts!" cried Dan, trying to stand firmly on the road and failing. He, too, hovered an inch or so above the earth.

"How can we be ghosts if we haven't died? We haven't even been born yet," Miranda said. "But we're luckier than Abby—at least we're not trapped at the ruin."

"I hope to heaven we're not trapped here," he said, and Miranda felt the panic rise in her again.

Okay, just accept it for now, Miranda told herself sternly as they floated along. *We have to worry about helping Abby—that's why we're here.* Miranda steeled herself for the task before her.

They drifted along, trying to catch up with the men. As they were approaching a small cluster of wooden buildings, the three men disappeared inside the main house. Miranda hovered and watched a girl carrying a basket of vegetables come out of the house and stand by the gate. She wore a soft gray dress that brushed her ankles. The collar on the dress was stiff and white, and lay in two points across her breast. On her head was a simple white bonnet, reminding Miranda of the ones she had seen Amish women wearing in Pennsylvania when she visited relatives there one summer. She wondered if this girl might have been one of Abby's friends.

The girl walked slowly, trailing her hand along the low fence that bordered the chicken yard by the house. Just as she passed by them, Dan waved and called out, "Hello!" But the girl did not turn. He wiped his hand across his face.

Miranda and Dan waited by the fence until Thomas emerged from the house. They drifted behind him again as he set off down the road.

Twentieth-century Garnet was a busy town, a historic landmark on the map of New England. In the summertime artists came to town and set up their easels on the common to paint the quaint old buildings along Main Street. Children bought ice cream cones from vendors on the street corners. Local restaurants offered "traditional" New England fare of meat pies, seafood, and chowder. Garnet in the summer pulsed with tourists, teenagers on bicycles, and the sounds of lawn mowers down the side streets and music from the street musicians on the common.

But Garnet of the seventeenth century was a very different place. Here, there were no busy streets, no motorcycles or cars. There was no music blaring from radios carried by kids on the sidewalks, no calls of street vendors peddling popcorn or hotdogs. The silence was what struck Miranda the most. She could hear birds as she walked, and animals scurrying in the bushes. She saw some deer watching from the side of the path. And there were no stores, as Abby had said, and no schools, no town hall, or hospital. The people she saw were all busy working, many of them doing unfamiliar tasks with tools she did not recognize. These people had a hard life to forge for themselves out of this new land. The artists, the ice cream stands, the restaurants would all be a long time coming.

The reality of having traveled through time in mere seconds threatened to overwhelm Miranda as she stared at the animals grazing on the village green. She breathed deeply as she drifted along, holding tightly to Dan's hand, soaking up impressions, and trying not to think.

All the houses they passed were unpainted, but some were quite large; whenever she had pictured Puritan New England—during a history lesson at school, for instance—Miranda had imagined the houses to have been very tiny log cabins. These were wooden houses, true, but of smooth planks rather than rough, round logs like the Lincoln Logs she had built playhouses with as a child. Every house along the green had a garden plot at the side and usually a chicken yard as well. The beans and corn grew tall in the sun, and the path that she and Dan skimmed along was dusty. Unfamiliar smells assaulted her nose: pungent wood smoke curling from every house, animals in the fields. The air, heavy and hot, smelled of pine.

Miranda shivered in the hot sun. Where were the snowdrifts of the Garnet winter she had left behind? She looked down and saw that although she and Dan had settled onto the path, they left no footprints in the dirt. Who was real and who was not in this strange, different Garnet?

The people they passed looked real. The villagers could not see Miranda or Dan, but they seemed to be real flesh and blood people who had their own lives and concerns—and never once thought of themselves as pages out of a history textbook or as exhibits in a museum. There was a tension about the villagers. A watchful wariness. *What are they afraid of?* wondered Miranda as she flew past. *Witches?* Some people talked in small groups—perhaps about the terrible fire that had claimed the lives of their neighbors. Others walked alone, on errands Miranda could not begin to imagine. There was no bank to go to. No dry cleaner or video store. No corner grocery. She tried to orient herself by imagining the Garnet she knew—they were moving along the edge of the common where Main Street was in the present. A few blocks over would be the high school. Susannah's house would be back where it looked like there were fields. Mrs. Wainwright's house on Elm Street would be built a few blocks to the north, where now there were only thick stands of trees. Miranda looked toward the hill, where her own house would be built in another hundred years. Dan's would be built even sooner—perhaps in another fifty years. So far the only thing Miranda had recognized was the Prindle House, and yet even that was missing its porch and the newer wing.

The women they passed wore bonnets, ruffs around their necks, shawls—even though the day was hot. Miranda stared openly at everyone, glad they couldn't see her. All had their heads covered, except for one young girl, perhaps eleven or twelve, who ambled toward them, swinging her bonnet by its long tie, her thick auburn hair held back from her face with a large tortoiseshell comb. She hummed as she passed them, settling the bonnet over her hair again as a group of men came into view farther down the lane.

"Amazing, isn't it?" asked Dan. He was

turning left and right as they drifted along, eager to take in all the details. "I wonder how it would feel to live here now? We'd be considered adults already, for one thing. That much about history I know. There wasn't any such thing as teenagers—I mean, I don't think anyone called people our age that until the end of the nineteenth century. I'd be working in the fields. We'd both be getting ready for marriage soon." He glanced down at Miranda and tried to joke. "So, how about it, my love. Willst thou marry me?"

She fluttered her eyelashes. "Why certainly, my good sir."

Ahead of them Thomas stopped outside a two-story dwelling built around a brick chimney. The roof was covered with wooden shingles and the windows were small, set with diamond-shaped panes of glass. It looked nothing like The Sassy Café.

"We're here," Miranda whispered. "Thomas's house."

Thomas opened the door and stepped inside. The door swung shut behind him.

"Should we knock?" asked Dan.

"Would they hear us?" Miranda walked up to the door and tentatively put her hand out. She touched the wood, felt the rough surface under her hand, but at the same time felt the matter change, as if the atoms were rearranging themselves and her hand slipped into the wood as if into water. She snatched her hand back in panic, their lightheartedness of only moments before entirely forgotten. *Please get me out of here*, she prayed. *I want to go home.* Never mind helping Abby. What could ghosts do, anyway?

Miranda saw that Dan was just as pale as she felt herself. "Did it hurt?" he asked.

"No. But it's—awful."

"Well, let's go if we're going." He motioned for her to go through the door. "Ladies first."

She hesitated, then drifted straight into the door, holding her breath. A split second later she emerged on the other side to find a thin young woman in a black dress and white apron, with braids coiled at her neck, staring at the door. Miranda gasped, hovering only inches from the woman. But after a moment the woman turned back to the huge fireplace. Something bubbled in a heavy black cauldron, the enticing aroma of sage wafting into the air. Miranda slowly exhaled.

A little girl dressed like her mother in black with a white apron played in the far corner of the room near a bed. She cradled what looked to Miranda like a bundle of corn husks, but which appeared to be the child's doll.

Keeping his voice low, just in case the people might hear them, Dan said, "The woman must be Sarah. And I bet the little girl is Charity." He glanced around quickly. "But I wonder where Thomas went?"

"I wish we could take something back with us," said Miranda. "For Abby." She reached out experimentally and brushed her finger against a tankard on the table. Her finger passed right through it. "But we can't. We don't make any impression here at all. How are we going to let Thomas know Abby is safe?"

"Try the phoenix," Dan suggested, and Miranda drew the stone figure out of her pocket. She raised it to her lips and blew the long sweet note into the air.

Little Charity dropped her doll. "What was that, Mama?"

Sarah looked around the room. "I don't know. Perhaps the boys have come back from the garden."

They had heard the whistle! Miranda closed her eyes and blew again.

"There it goes again, Mama! And the boys aren't here at all." Charity sounded frightened. "It came from over by the door."

Sarah walked toward them then and opened the door. She stepped outside. Miranda held her breath. After a moment Sarah came back, closing the door firmly behind her. "It must have been someone out in the lane," she said, returning to the fireplace. Charity settled down with her doll again.

Miranda and Dan hovered near the door. "So they can hear the whistle. But how can we tell them about Abby?" moaned Miranda. "I wish I knew how to toot out a message in Morse code."

"Morse code hasn't been invented yet," Dan whispered back. "Anyway, you tried. That's what we'll have to tell Abby." They hovered silently, watching Sarah's dinner preparations. After another moment, Dan added, "But I wish I'd brought a camera. Pictures of this place would help Abby feel less homesick."

"Yeah, not to mention the great photo essay you could do."

Miranda looked around her, willing herself to remember details so she could report to Abby. It was a wonderful room, she thought, filled with an astonishing array of things—a museum exhibit come alive. There were no "do not touch" signs posted, and the utensils and furnishings were bright and new rather than darkened with age. This was a real house, a place where a family lived. How Mrs. Hooton would love to see all this! For a fleeting second Miranda wondered whether there could possibly be invisible visitors from the distant future in her own house in Garnet, looking around, marveling at the "quaint" lifestyle of the late twentieth century.

The enormous fireplace with its pots and kettles on wooden crossbars was the main feature. The beams above were full of hooks from which bundles of dried herbs hung, and not only herbs—dried corn and apples dangled from strings; huge sides of ham and bacon had been strung high inside the fireplace to smoke. Near the fireplace was the long table flanked by benches and two chairs at either end. There was a bench next to the fireplace, with a hinged seat. Miranda recalled having seen one in the Hootons' museum. It was called a settle, and the compartment under the seat was for storing linens or clothes. A narrow, enclosed staircase led upstairs from one corner by the fireplace.

Miranda and Dan floated together toward the far wall. Shelves contained bowls and rough-looking metal dishes. "They're pewter," Dan whispered. "We have them in the museum. No one here knows about lead poisoning yet." They moved toward the fireplace, passing the small and large spinning wheels under the narrow window and the loom for weaving, which took up one entire corner.

Sarah reached above her head and pinched sprigs from a dried rosemary plant hanging from the ceiling beam. She threw the herb into the bubbling stew and the aroma from the broth made Miranda's stomach rumble. Then a low door in the back wall opened, and Thomas ducked through with a small boy on his shoulders. Another boy came in behind them. Thomas set the child down and latched the door. She noticed that both little boys wore shoes of leather decorated by large buckles. At least *something* looked just as the history books showed.

"They must be Daniel and Nicholas," breathed Dan.

Thomas walked across the room to Sarah, who quickly wiped her hands on a coarse cloth, her eyes on his face. He grabbed her by the shoulders and pulled her roughly to him. Her arms came up to stroke his back, then tightened around him in a hug.

After a moment, he set her away from him and sank onto the settle. "Charity?" he said, "Where is a hug for thy father?" The little girl left her doll and came to him.

"I missed thee," Sarah said. "It seemed a long time."

Sarah's eyes were sorrowful as she ladled stew into heavy pewter bowls and set the bowls around the table. She placed a large loaf of dark bread covered with a white cloth on a board. Then she poured some amber liquid into a great tankard and set that on the table as well. "We had best eat," she said. "This is another sad day, but at least we are together, the five of us. That's something to be thankful for."

"Daniel and Nicholas," called Thomas. "Come to the table."

"I wish we could eat something, too," whispered Dan. "It smells so good." They watched the family gather around the long table for the prayer.

"Lord," began Thomas in a deep, resonant voice, "we ask Thy blessing on this food that Thou in Thy abundant mercy hast given. We know it is not by good food and contentments of this world alone that we preserve our life and health. It is by Thy strength and Thy grace that we survive this time of grief and loss. We ask, Lord, for Thy protection against future perils. We ask for Thy blessing on our souls, and on the souls of our family and friend who did not survive the fire." When he paused, everyone around the table remained silent, heads bowed. After a moment he added softly, "Please protect my sister, young Abigail, wherever she may be. Amen."

Sarah and the children echoed him. "Amen."

But before they could begin their simple meal, there came a heavy knock upon the door. Thomas rose from his chair to answer. "Why, it's Henry Mather. Come in, Neighbor."

A thickset man wearing a black hat and a long tunic like Thomas's entered and nodded to the family. "Goodwife," he said to Sarah, removing his hat to reveal a bald head. "Forgive the intrusion at mealtime. Thomas? I have important news. We have found—"

"Is it Abigail?" Thomas grabbed the man's arms. "Henry, have you found my sister?"

Henry hesitated. "No, I am sorry we have not. But I must speak about the fire, Thomas."

"Please, do sit and try the soup," Sarah invited him. " 'Tis a vegetable broth flavored with pork. I know you must be hungry."

Henry set his hat on the settle, nodding tiredly. He sank onto the bench next to Daniel and smiled at the children, who greeted him politely. Sarah ladled some soup into a bowl for him, handed him a hunk of bread, and passed him the heavy mug. All the family drank from the one tankard, Miranda noted.

Henry drank deeply and sighed as he set the mug down on the table again. "Ah, that is fine ale, Goodwife."

She thanked him. They ate in silence, and the atmosphere in the room grew heavier. Thomas waited until the man had finished before speaking. He said, "Perhaps you children would like to play out in the lane for a time?"

"Oh, aye," they chorused and left promptly, Charity dragging the cornhusk doll.

Thomas turned to Henry. "Now, Henry. What would you have us know?"

Henry cleared his throat. "Clara was berrying in the woods behind the Prindle House when she saw the Indian woman kneeling by a small fire and muttering an incantation. Her shack is there, you know, on the hill, and Clara would not go too close. But she came to tell me that Willow's eyes were wild. As my daughter in all innocence passed by, hidden by the trees, Willow looked up and cast her eye upon the girl. As she did so, the small fire leapt up and caught some dry leaves—and the Indian had to hurry to put out the flames lest the whole forest be burned." His voice cracked. "Thomas, I'm telling you, I fear that woman.

People are saying now that she cast her eye on your parents' house and similarly started a fire. I think they must be right." Henry looked at his neighbors and raised his hands, palms up in a gesture of supplication. "'Tis frightening to know such evil is among us. But how else could the roof catch so suddenly as it did unless the devil were about?"

Sarah's face was very pale.

Henry glanced over his shoulder as if searching for an unseen presence and lowered his voice. "Josiah Prindle swears he saw a large bird on the roof of his house just before William left to join your family for the meal. The bird flew along with him and rested atop your family's roof as William entered the house. It was a devil bird, Josiah believes. A spirit sent by the Indian to harm poor William."

Thomas sprang suddenly to life. He stood next to Henry and placed a hand on his broad shoulder. "I thank you for coming to tell us this news."

"But, Thomas, we must act." Henry thumped his fist on the table. "You owe it to your family and to your neighbors to help extinguish the evil flame among us. Both your parents are dead now, man—and your three sisters. One body cannot even be found—can you tell me that is not a sign more than anything else of witchcraft? The Indian must have spirited Abigail's body away—to use for only the Devil-knows-what infernal purpose!"

The back of Miranda's neck prickled.

"The men are assembling now. We must act quickly, my friend." Henry reached for his hat.

Dan shook his head. "What total bull," he said loudly. But of course no one but Miranda heard him. "Let's get out of here."

CHAPTER
SIXTEEN

BUT MIRANDA didn't budge. "Wait a minute."

"Godspeed," Thomas said to Henry Mather, seeing him out. Then he closed the door gently and turned to his wife. "Oh, Sarah."

"It's starting again," she whispered and tightened her fists in her skirts.

"As if we didn't already have enough to bear."

"I grieve for thee, dear Thomas." She reached out her hands to him. "I know how precious thy family was to thee, how precious Abigail was especially. But remember, she no longer suffers. She has gone on to a new life. They all have. It's what we must believe."

Miranda's heart pounded hard. A better life? Had she? Was it? She remembered her promise to Abby. She must try to comfort Thomas.

"Thomas!" Miranda called, floating across the room to him. She tried to grasp his arm. "Listen to me. Abby *didn't* die! Please don't look so awful. She's all right, she's living with us now. Willow gave her a little statue, and that's what saved her from the fire."

"Get back here," hissed Dan. "What are you doing?"

Thomas shook his head at Sarah. He didn't notice Miranda at all, though she hovered at his side. "If 'tis true what our neighbor says, and the fire was no accident but brought on by an evil witch's spell, then justice must be done."

"No, Thomas, don't," implored Sarah. "Thou knowst it must have been an accident. There has been no rain in so long, the fields and woods are dry as bone. The roof of the house might easily have caught by a spark from the chimney. Do not follow those who would chase out and accuse a poor woman of"—her voice dropped—"witchcraft."

Miranda tried again, drifting this way and that around Thomas and Sarah. "Willow wasn't evil! She helped Abby. Oh, Thomas, don't!" she implored.

Thomas passed his hand across his face.

Then he looked down and seemed to meet Miranda's eyes. "I—I almost feel . . ." His voice dwindled, and he gazed toward the window.

"What is it, Thomas?" asked Sarah.

"Abigail?" he whispered. "There is a— presence here. I sense it."

Miranda clutched Dan. "Abigail is safe," she repeated urgently, willing him to understand. Then she remembered the phoenix and fished it from her pocket. She raised it to her lips and blew. The long note hung in the air, an unseen messenger.

Thomas gasped and grabbed his wife's shoulder. "Did you hear the unearthly cry? It is the Devil's music. Oh, dear Lord, it isn't Abigail at all," he moaned, looking around the room with great fear in his eyes. "Lord, protect us from the evil that surrounds us."

"But it's not evil!" cried Miranda. "Oh, Dan, what can we do to make him understand?"

"Nothing," he whispered back. "Let's get out of here."

"I heard the sound before," confessed Sarah in a hoarse whisper. "When I was alone with Charity. I thought it came from the road."

"No, it was in this room." Thomas thumped his fist hard on the table. "It is a sign, Sarah! We must discover whether the Indian has spirited Abigail away. I assure thee, I shall not be the one to judge her. The law shall do that. But we must find her in the woods and lock her up so she can do no more damage to our family and our land."

He moved resolutely to the door. Miranda could hear voices outside now, calling for him. "Dost thou hear them, Sarah?" he asked. "Listen."

"Oh, Thomas, no. Grieve at home with us, but do not wreak vengeance on an innocent woman."

"We do not know she is innocent," he snapped.

Sarah bit her lip as he reached for the musket that hung on nails above the door. Then she called the children and they came running around the side of the house. She gathered them against her skirts and stood watching.

Down the road came ten or fifteen men and boys, all calling for Thomas to join them in routing the Devil from Garnet. Dan floated over to the door. "These people are crazy," he muttered in disgust. "Let's *go*, Mandy."

Miranda felt sick at the thought of what the men meant to do. "I don't think they're crazy. I think they're scared to death." She held the phoenix tightly. Its cool, hard weight in her hand made her feel calmer. "Maybe we can warn Willow."

"*How?*" demanded Dan. "We can't help anyone—not Abby, not Thomas, and not Willow." But he floated behind Miranda as she edged around Sarah and the children, out into the dusty lane.

With flutters of panic in her stomach, Miranda watched the men stamping off toward the common. She looked back and saw Sarah's face at the small front window, fearful and sad.

Miranda and Dan flew along as fast and as high as they could, skimming just beneath the lower branches of the trees. *Too bad we can't soar above everything—like birds*, Miranda thought. But they could not move much faster than the men themselves, though now they were drawing abreast of the angry mob assembled near the stocks in the common.

The men stopped to discuss how best to organize themselves to trap and capture the witch. Miranda and Dan flew right on toward the Prindle House and the burned ruin. Beyond the house and the ruin lay the woods. They drifted silently among the old trees, following the path of moss until they came to a clearing. The sharp scent of pine surrounded them.

Miranda rubbed her fists into her eyes.

What she saw before her looked at first sight like an illustration from a legend: a small shack built of wood and animal skins stood amidst the birch and pine trees. At one side of the shack flowed a stream, dotted with rocks. On the other side of the shack a garden had been planted. Tall stalks of corn stood at the back along the natural fence of blueberry bushes. Rows of vegetables grew in leafy green abundance. Directly outside the door of the shack was a circle of stones and a spit, from which hung a black pot. "For the witch's brew," Dan murmured. Smells of pungent herbs hung in the air.

Miranda snorted. She moved forward first. "Hello?" she called. "Is anyone home?"

"She won't be able to hear you," said Dan.

Miranda walked around the clearing, taking in all the details. It was a peaceful place, with dappled sunlight falling through the trees and water rushing along in the stream. Birds chirped and unseen animals chattered from the forest.

Then the skin-covered door of the shack was swept aside and the woman emerged, holding a basket. She was tall and dark and younger than Miranda had expected. She was wearing a long black dress like the other women Miranda had seen in town. But her feet were bare and her black hair, streaked with threads of gray, hung in two long braids down her back. Dan lingered by the shelter of pine trees, but Miranda floated straight over to her.

"We've come to warn you," she began. "You're in trouble."

The woman walked to her garden and squatted among the herbs and flowers. She began picking and gathering them into bunches, tying the ends of the stems with string and snipping the string at the knot with a sharp knife.

Miranda moved forward. "You must go away from here—and fast. Men are coming, and they think you're a witch! Oh, can't you hear us, either?"

"Why should she?" asked Dan. "No one else can."

Miranda shrugged. Despite her insistence that she didn't believe in witches, she found herself hoping this woman would have the special power to sense their presence. Miranda drifted into the garden and crouched near the woman. "Please hear us!" She waved her hands around, trying to stir up the air to create a breeze. But the woman, her head bowed, continued snipping and tying the herbs into small bundles and placing them in her basket.

"Abby said Willow uses herbs and flowers

as medicine," Miranda told Dan. "She heals people."

"Then how dare they come up here now and try to hurt her?" Behind them, back through the trees, they could hear the sounds of the men approaching. Miranda's heart beat faster as Willow lifted her head to listen. Willow's calm expression sharpened. "Go away," Dan cried. "They're coming to lock you up!"

Willow cocked her head, then resumed her work with the herbs and flowers. She didn't seem afraid, didn't seem to have any idea that the group of men meant her harm.

"She probably thinks it's a hunting party," Dan said grimly. "Let's go—I can't bear to stay and watch." He turned to drift through the clearing, back along the path the way they'd come. "Come on, Mandy. You don't want to watch them capture her."

She put her hands on her hips. "How can you just leave her?"

Dan shook his head. "I don't see what we can do, Mandy. Remember, all this happened three hundred years ago. It's over and done with—it's history. We can't change anything. I just want to get out of here and go back home."

Miranda watched Willow lay the bundles in

her basket. Rose and thyme and other plants Miranda could not identify scented the warm air in a smell that was real, was here and now, no matter *when* now was. She pressed her lips together stubbornly. She had to try to make Willow know the danger she was in. It wouldn't be long before the men burst into the clearing and seized her. She would be carried roughly away from her peaceful clearing, then locked in a cell somewhere in town. A judge would find her guilty of burning down Abby's house and killing her family and William. She would be branded a witch and killed right out in the common. Miranda couldn't bear to stay and watch, but she couldn't bear to leave, knowing the men would come.

She hovered near Willow like a guardian angel without any real power. *If only I could make you see me,* she thought desperately. *If only I could make you hear. . . .*

The phoenix! She took it hurriedly from her pocket and raised it to her lips. She blew, and the long note soared out into the hot summer air. Willow lifted her head again and listened. The men's arrival was imminent, but still she must think it would be a party of hunters, out for stag or rabbit or grouse. No danger to her.

Then Miranda blew the whistle again, and

Willow's face darkened. She stood up hurriedly, leaving the basket in the garden, and ran to her shack. "Don't go in there!" cried Miranda, floating toward her. "It's not safe." Over and over she blew the whistle.

Willow stood in the doorway, staring out at the clearing. Her eyes were wide and black. "I know this music," Willow said uncertainly. She glanced left and right. "Can it be spirits? Why do you come to me?" She turned and ducked into the shack.

Miranda floated inside after her. The interior of the shack was dim. There didn't seem to be any furniture at all, just mats of woven cloth and piles of animal furs. Several earthenware bowls lay on the packed ground by the entrance. Miranda blew the phoenix again urgently. "Get out of here," she cried, and then blew again.

Willow looked around in desperation, grabbed up some furs and a pouch with long leather ties, stowed her knife in the pouch, and slung it around her neck. Then she slipped out the door, Miranda at her side blowing again and again the warning note. *Run, run, run,* the phoenix seemed to sing.

And at last, Willow ran. She left the clearing faster than Miranda could have run, along the stream, then across the stream to another path. Then she disappeared amidst the foliage just as the mass of angry Garnet citizens stormed into the clearing. Miranda gasped when she saw their guns and swords. Then she remembered they could not see her.

Across the clearing Dan waited for her in the shadows.

The men, led by stout Mr. Prindle, swept through the garden, trampling the flowers and herbs. Mr. Mather was there, too, and Thomas. They surged toward the shack. Miranda shrank behind the tree, shocked that men she had seen in the town less than an hour ago could have become such marauders.

William's father hoisted Willow's basket on his sword. "The witch is here!" he cried. "Find her!"

"*Was* here, you mean," said Henry Mather, peering into the hut. "But she will likely return." He settled himself on a log outside the door. "I can wait. Aye, I can wait."

"I think we should search in the woods," said a young, eager boy about Miranda's age. His red hair stood on end and his eyes gleamed with excitement. "She may be trying to run away—probably heard us coming. If we hurry, we may still catch her."

He started off with a few other boys exactly in the direction Willow had gone. Miranda's heart pounded harder. She raised the phoenix again to her lips and blew it as hard as she could. The long note soared out, suspended for a moment in the clearing. The men froze.

Thomas sagged. "Again! We heard it back at our house, my wife and I."

"It is the sign of the Devil!" Mr. Prindle shouted.

"It is the witch!"

"She means to harm us!"

"She has turned herself into a bird—look there on the bush!"

"She is hiding here, watching us, I can sense it!"

The men drew together, fearful and dangerous. Mr. Prindle raised his musket and shot into the air. Thomas did the same. Miranda cringed and floated across the clearing to Dan.

"Good thinking!" Dan hugged her. It was so good to feel his arms, real and strong around her. "Brave Mandy."

"It won't stop them," she sighed, as the men seemed to recover their wits and fanned out to search the woods.

"No, but you slowed them up. You got Willow to leave, and now she's had some time to hide. She probably knows all sorts of places these guys don't."

Miranda blew the phoenix whistle several more times, just to watch the men stop, their faces blanch, their stocky bodies tremble. Finally she stowed the phoenix back in her pocket. Dan led the way down the path back to the ruin.

"Do you think we saved her?" asked Miranda when they stood again among the rubble of Abby's home. "I can't bear not knowing."

She was shivering in the late afternoon sun. A cool breeze began, then whipped itself into a wind. Dark clouds gathered and it looked like rain.

"We gave her a chance, at least," said Dan. "That is, *you* did."

Miranda walked around the charred ruins of the house, marveling at how firmly her boots touched the earth now that she was back inside the barrier of wind. It was a relief not to be floating anymore. The bundle of their old-time clothes lay by the rock where she had left it. She picked it up and looked across the rubble to where the Prindle House stood, new and sturdy and strong. She wanted only to be back home, to see her parents again, to see the

Prindle House as it was in her own time, old and rickety and ready for repair. But first they had to tell Abby what had happened with Willow. They had to tell Abby they had not been able to let Thomas know that his little sister was safe.

Abby listened with her head bowed. Miranda ached to comfort her, but there were no words.

Finally she reached for Abby's hand. "We've been here for hours, it seems. And now it's going to pour. Let's go."

But Abby was shaking her head. "I'm not going back," she said, raising her head at last. Her eyes were dazed.

"But Abby," said Miranda. "We have to."

"There's nothing for me in your time. I can't spend the rest of eternity moving on and on and on." She sank onto a charred beam and put her head in her hands. "And there's nothing for me in my own time, as you and Dan have proven today. I've always known the way out, but for centuries I've been too much a coward to take it."

"Take it? Take what?" asked Miranda. "What are you talking about?"

"Take the only escape route out of a life that's really no life at all." Abby looked directly into their eyes. Her own were full of tears, but resolute. "I want most of all to be with my family and William."

"But they're dead." Dan's voice was brutal. "Burned to death. *Dead*, Abby!"

"That's right." She nodded. "And so must I be, if I want to be with them again."

Miranda gasped. "Then you're talking about suicide? Abby, you can't mean you're going to try to kill yourself."

"Why not?"

"Don't be stupid," said Dan. "You're going to wish us home. Now!"

But Abby walked toward a clump of toadstools growing beneath a tree. "Look, it may not even work. I mean, can a ghost die again? But these are very poisonous. I have to try. It's the best way. Thomas might find my body. He can bury me with my mother and father and sisters. I'll be with William again."

"Stop her!" cried Miranda, running over. "Don't let her try to eat them."

A small procession of men was coming toward them from the woods. The trees behind them swayed back and forth in the wind. Miranda recognized the figure in front as Thomas. The men were empty-handed. This small band had not tracked Willow down to capture her, and Miranda sighed inwardly with relief even as she struggled with Abby. She hoped that the other search parties had also found no one.

"Thomas!" screamed Abby. "Wait! Here I am!" She tried to run to him, heedless of the wind barrier, but was swept into the gale again and hurled back onto the ground.

Dan and Miranda helped her to her feet. "You'd think after three hundred years of trying," he said, "you'd learn."

"Wish us home," Miranda implored her. "Do it now."

"But I want my family!" cried Abby, her hair whipping across her face in the wind.

Miranda yelled back at her. "Abigail Chandler, your family is *dead, dead, dead!* But mine is alive, and I want to see them again. You may not value your life, but Dan and I value ours." Her words were harsh; she meant them to be. "Damn it, Abby, you've lived longer already than Dan and I ever will, and you don't appreciate it at all. I wish you'd grow up."

"I want to grow up, too," hissed Abby. "But I can't. That's the problem."

Abby's face was set with a determination Miranda had not seen before, and she felt a new stab of fear. What could they do if Abby really did refuse to wish them home again? The three of them stood in the charred rubble, ash eddying around them, stirred by the wind.

Abby stubbornly folded her arms across her chest. But at least she wasn't trying to get the toadstools now. Miranda glanced at Dan. What were they going to do if they couldn't convince Abby? There had to be a way.

Miranda's hand crept into her pocket to stroke the cold stone of the phoenix. As before, the feel of it calmed her. And with the new calm came inspiration. Slowly, she drew the phoenix out and held it up. "Look, Abby," she said. "It's you. I mean, you're sort of a phoenix, too. Did you ever think of it that way?"

At Abby's uncomprehending stare, Miranda nodded. "Well, it's true. You are. In the legend, the bird dies in the fire, right? And then it's reborn out of the flames and lives on. But it doesn't live on as its old self—it becomes a new phoenix, with a new life."

"That's right," said Dan. He took the phoenix from Miranda and pressed it into Abby's hand. "You did that, too! You died in the fire, but Willow's statue gave you a chance to start again. You're dead in this time. Just a ghost. But that's okay, because you can come home with us now, and start again."

"Home to what?" Abby's eyes narrowed.

She was again the Abby that Miranda knew so well, sarcastic and hostile. "It's no real life there, either. I'm tired of never growing, never changing, being drawn back here just to sit and cry, then going back again, just existing on and on." Her shoulders sagged, and when she spoke next her voice was very soft, hardly audible over the wind. "I would rather die right now than go on that way. I don't *want* to be a phoenix anymore."

Her simple words stirred something deep inside Miranda that all Abby's shouting had failed to reach. Could the solution to Abby's troubles be as simple as deciding *not* to be a phoenix? The first raindrops began to fall. "Come home now," she told Abby. "I need some time to think things through. But maybe I can still help, after all. We can try again."

Abby looked down at the cold stone phoenix in her hand. "Without this bird," she said slowly, "everything would have ended for me in the house that day. Charred bone—" She turned the words over experimentally in her mouth. "Like the others. That's all I'd be. But I'm not, am I?" She looked up at them. "I'm not."

They shook their heads.

Abby gazed at them both with a blank, faraway look in her pale eyes. She seemed to be coming to some decision, for she nodded to herself after a moment. "All right," she said. "I'll take you home." She reached out her hands to them. Miranda's heart beat faster; she had been truly frightened that this moment would never come.

"Close your eyes," Abby whispered.

Miranda glanced hastily around her for one last look before she obeyed. Here on the grass at the edge of the woods, it could be any time. The rain pelting down around them now could fall in any age. Then almost immediately the rain vanished, the air grew dense around them, almost unbearably stifling, then thinned again, and turned cooler, cold. It was this cold air that Miranda gasped into her lungs just as the smell changed to that of pizza, and she heard Abby's words, "Open your eyes now. We're home."

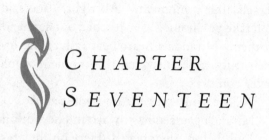

CHAPTER SEVENTEEN

"MY GOODNESS, I thought you girls had gone home already!" Mrs. Hooton exclaimed as the three time travelers, silent and shaken, slowly walked down the steps from the museum wing into the front hall. "But since you're here, you're welcome to share our bedtime snack. Leftover pizza."

Miranda checked her watch, then clenched Dan's hand. They had traveled so far together, she could not believe so little time had passed. She couldn't bear to leave before they had a chance to talk. He squeezed her fingers, willing her to stay, needing her closeness as she needed his. But then Miranda saw Abby's stricken face and slowly shook her head. "No, thanks. Abby and I had better get home."

"Well, it is getting late." Mrs. Hooton saw

them to the door. As they started down the front steps, she called after them. "Oh, would you girls like to come along with Dan to meet me at the Prindle House tomorrow after school? The witchcraft exhibit is just about ready. You three can have a sneak preview, if you like, before we open it to the public."

"That'll be nice," Miranda answered faintly and hurried across the snowy street after Abby.

Abby was withdrawn as they sat in the living room with Helen and Philip over their bedtime hot chocolate. Miranda felt a terrible urge to talk to her parents, to tell them about everything that had happened. But one glance at Abby's set face made her press her lips together hard. This was Abby's drama—she herself was in the wings while Abby stood center stage. There was a certain relief, too, in leaving the explanations to Abby. Miranda sipped her drink, remembering the fragrant stew in Sarah's cauldron.

Abby drained her cup, then looked up at Philip. "Where do you think we go when we die?"

He peered into his mug. "Helen, what did you put in here?"

Abby didn't smile. "I just wonder, that's all."

Miranda tried to catch Abby's eye, but Abby leaned toward Philip, waiting intently.

"I don't know, of course," said Philip. He set his mug on the coffee table. "People believe different things. It depends on what your religion teaches—"

"No, that can't be right." Abby cut him off. "I've been to dozens of churches and synagogues. Religions think they know, but I need *proof*. How can I get absolute proof?"

Helen laughed uncertainly. "Abby, theologians, philosophers, scientists, and just about everybody else for thousands of years—no, certainly much longer than that—have all been wondering the exact same thing you are, and no one has ever found proof that everyone will accept as proof. Faith is an important element of all religions for precisely that reason. I, for one, believe there is a God and a heaven."

"And when you die you'll be with all your family and friends who died before you?"

"I'm not sure I'd go that far, personally," said Helen. "But I know many religions would say yes. And it certainly is a comforting thought."

"So the only way to know for sure is to die, I suppose," said Abby dully.

"Probably," said Helen. She looked questioningly at Miranda as Abby returned to her hot chocolate. Miranda just shrugged. No one spoke for some time; the only sound in the room was the clink of their spoons against the mugs.

Then Abby stood up. "Excuse me. I've had enough—and I'm feeling sort of dizzy. I'm going to bed."

Helen rose hastily. "Let me feel your forehead, honey. Are you coming down with something?"

"No—" Abby waited while Helen placed a hand on her brow. "I'm just tired." She headed for the stairs.

"Let her go, Helen," said Philip, and Helen sat down again.

"What's wrong with Abby, Mandy? Do you know?" she asked.

Miranda shrugged. How to tell them of Abby's despair? How to give them an accurate account of how Abby tried to go back before the fire, of her failure, of her longing to die so that she might at last rejoin her family? At least she hadn't been able to try the poison mushrooms.

Miranda choked on her hot chocolate. Abby had not, after all, been able to kill herself in the past. But nothing prevented her from trying to commit suicide here.

"Excuse me, too," Miranda said, shoving

back her chair. "I'll go talk to her, see if any-thing's wrong."

As she hurried out of the room, she heard her father's soft voice. "It's just great how friendly the girls have been to each other these past couple of days. Maybe things really will work out for us after all."

"Oh, I hope so," said Helen fervently. "It would be so wonderful. . . ."

Miranda sucked in her breath and ran up-stairs. Nothing could ever work out if Abby were already dead. She barged into Abby's bed-room without knocking. "Abby? Abby?" But the room was empty.

Cold fear plunged into Miranda's stomach. The bathroom! Razor blades or who knew what in the medicine chest? But when she ran down the hall to check, that room was empty, too. Miranda put her hands to her face.

She ran to her own room and flung herself onto the bed. Then she noticed Abby in the corner window seat, legs drawn up tightly be-neath her.

"Oh, Abby!"

"What's the matter? Seen a ghost?"

"I thought you were going to—"

"Kill myself?" Abby nodded. "I was think-ing about it. But I'm a ninny. A great big cow-ard." Her voice cracked with angry tears.

"Maybe it wouldn't work anyway. Maybe I wouldn't die even if I tried. But in order to know, I need someone to push me over the cliff, to pull the trigger, to knock the chair out from under me once my head is in the noose—"

"Abby, stop it—please!"

Abby's eyes glittered as she hugged her legs. "I need you to put the poison berries in my tea, or stab me with a dagger. Will you do it, Mandy? You with your safe home and loving family and normal life? Will you do it so I can get back to my own parents—and William?"

Miranda stared at Abby. She saw the twitch at the side of Abby's mouth, that old sardonic, unpleasant smirk. Miranda's pity dissolved. Her voice when she spoke was sharp. "You know I won't. And only someone as selfish as you would ever ask such a thing. Just leave me out of it. I won't shove you down the stairs or shoot your brains out, much as I'd sometimes like to. But listen—last year Mither sprained her back and had to take some pretty strong painkillers. I bet she has some left. Go check the bathroom. Take a couple pills and you'll fall asleep. Take ten—you fall down unconscious. Take the whole bottle, Abby, why don't you? Take it and see if maybe you really *will* die!"

Abby's smirky, superior grin vanished and

her eyes filled with tears. Miranda jumped off her bed and stamped right over to the window seat. She shouted into the other girl's face, "Yes, you'll die at last! And what an easy way to go. Even a coward like you can manage it!" She held up her hand when Abby tried to speak. "I know what you'll say next. You'll want me to be the one to pour you the cup of water. No way. This is something you'll do all by yourself. But I'll get my parents to come up and kiss you before you fall asleep. I won't tell them it's good-bye, of course, because they'd rush you to the hospital and pump your stomach, and we know you wouldn't want that."

Her voice rose scornfully. "So they'll kiss you good night, and when they go downstairs again they'll say what I just heard them saying a few minutes ago. How happy they are that you're living with us, how they hope you and I will be friends, how much they want you to stay. Of course you won't hear them, because you'll already have sunk into a stupor. But you wouldn't care, anyway, right? Because we don't matter to you. All you want is to die—on the off chance you'll meet up with people who died three hundred years ago." Miranda broke off to catch her breath and glared at Abby. "All these years of life you've had, Abby—and I don't think you've appreciated one minute. All you've been doing is wishing you *weren't* alive. Well, you don't deserve to be."

She stopped at last, shocked at herself. Abby's head was bowed now and tears dropped onto her knees. Miranda felt tears start in her own eyes. After a long pause, she spoke up grudgingly. "I—I'm sorry. You wouldn't really die from the pills, Abby. In fact, I don't really think we even have any more. But even if we did, and even if you took the whole bottle, I'd be on the phone for an ambulance before you finished swallowing."

Abby lifted her head and threw her arms around Miranda. "Oh, Mandy," she sobbed. "I know I'm awful. I don't really want to die— I just can't bear going on like this. How long does that legend say phoenixes live? Isn't it five hundred years? If I'm a phoenix as you say, does that mean two hundred more years for me? I hate living on and on and never changing, while the people I care about die. I hate going back to the ruin all the time, just to cry there for all I've lost."

"I know." Miranda sat on the window seat next to Abby. She was trying to think back to the moment in the ruin, trying to remember the idea that had risen out of the ashes. Abby had said then she didn't want to be a phoenix. And yet she had no choice. Or did she?

She contemplated the pale girl. "You *look* just like a normal person. You were born like everyone. You lived a normal life—until the moment you should have died. Then something magical happened, and you didn't really die at all. It happened because of one special thing you had that no one else in the world had. The phoenix. Somehow it gave you another chance."

"Rebirth out of the ashes," murmured Abby. "But no chance for a normal life."

"I wonder," mused Miranda. She turned to look out the window into darkness. She could sense the deep blankets of snow, though she couldn't see them.

That night she dreamed about flying.

The next day Miranda wandered through her classes in a fog. She remembered how it felt to drift above the ground. She couldn't concentrate on her work. She had Abby on her mind.

When the final bell rang she sighed with relief. Soon she and Abby and Dan were crunching along Main Street, then around the corner to the Prindle House. A backhoe was parked in the vacant lot, shrouded with snow.

The ash and rubble of the ruin seemed more real. "Soon this will be a parking lot," Miranda marveled. "Can you believe it?"

Mrs. Hooton called to them from the porch of the Prindle House. Mrs. Wainwright stepped out from behind her and waved. On the porch, Dan introduced Abby to his great-aunt, then they all went inside.

Miranda looked around with interest as they walked through the old house, but there wasn't much to see. The wide wooden floorboards were covered with white dropcloths. Wallpaper hung in tatters. Paint buckets and plastering tools lay on planks atop sawhorses. Mrs. Wainwright led them up the narrow staircase to a newly painted bedroom. The wooden floor gleamed with fresh wax. Glass cases had been installed under the window, and a banner above read WITCHCRAFT IN GARNET?

"Welcome to the Witch House exhibit," Mrs. Wainwright said, motioning them to step closer and look. "Your parents have done a stellar job, Dan."

"Take your time." Mrs. Hooton smiled. "We'll be downstairs with the carpenters."

Miranda, Abby, and Dan crowded close to peer into the first case. A brief history on easy-to-read tagboard cards told about the hysteria that had gripped late seventeenth-century New England. An etching showed a woman tied to a chair attached to a plank held above a pond, and the caption explained that this was a ducking stool. Once used throughout New England as a punishment for wives who nagged their husbands, the ducking stool was utilized in Garnet during the witchcraft hysteria as a test to prove whether or not the accused were truly a witch. A real witch, people believed, could not drown. So if the accused drowned, then she was not guilty.

"Oh, wow," said Dan. "Not guilty, but dead anyway?"

"Looks like it," said Miranda, frowning. "I wonder if it says anything here about Willow?" She gazed down into the case, trying to read the old documents listing the accused persons and their sentences.

Dan shook his head. "I checked. Her name isn't there."

Abby moved on to the second case. She looked inside. After a moment she called to them to come look. Her voice sounded ragged.

They peered down at a torn, yellowed page from an old newspaper. "Look at the date," whispered Abby. "1755—a year before I came here to live with Matilda and Tobias Prindle. It's a letter written by Tobias himself."

Miranda frowned at the faded, oddly formed letters. "What does it say? I can't read it."

But Abby had no difficulty.

"The sins of the fathers weigh heavily upon this family. We are besmirched by the stain of our ancestors' Guilt. They who so willingly and with vigor participated in the insanity that plagued our Town some sixty years ago have left a Shadow upon all generations to follow. We cannot hope to be forgiven in the eyes of God in Heaven without first atoning here on Earth, and to our fellow Men. I therefore offer freely and without obligation Monetary Restitution to the surviving families whose members were accused and executed for the Crime of Witchcraft in Garnet. I acknowledge the responsibility of my ancestor, Josiah Prindle, in leading these Baseless Accusations, and hope to diminish the Guilt that stains my Soul and the Souls of my family by this act of most humble atonement—"

She stopped. "And the rest is torn away."

"It's enough, though, isn't it?" asked Miranda. "We know that William's father went off the deep end, but at least it sounds like later generations of Prindles were sorry."

"It's sad," murmured Dan. He put his arm around Abby's thin shoulders. "Tobias felt so ashamed, even though he hadn't been born when it was going on."

"Do you think that's how come you landed so far in the future?" asked Miranda. "The phoenix sent you on to a time when people didn't believe in witches anymore—so you would be safer."

"Safer, maybe," said Abby. "But still always on the run."

They looked at each other, then wandered through the rest of the exhibit without another word. The sound of a carpenter's drill led them down the steep stairs to Dan's mother and Mrs. Wainwright, who were watching the carpenters replacing rotten floorboards in a back room. "Ready to go?" asked Mrs. Hooton. She put on her coat and scarf. Mrs. Wainwright accompanied them to the front door, chatting cheerfully about the renovations.

"Thanks for letting us in to the exhibit early," said Dan. "It's awesome."

"But horrible," said Miranda. "I've never heard of anything so stupid as that ducking stool in my whole life."

Abby wound her scarf over her pale hair. "People were different then," she said in her quiet voice.

"Oh, don't you believe it for a minute, my girl," said Mrs. Wainwright. "That's a mistake we often make when thinking about history. But you can be sure the people in old Garnet were no different from us at all. Their ways may have been different—and some of their fears—but at heart they were like us. They hoped for what we all hope for. Good health, good friends, a family to love, enough food, and a safe place to live. They lived their lives day to day, just the same as you and I." She opened the door and they stepped out into the cold again. "That's really all we ever can do."

They said good-bye then, and Mrs. Hooton drove carefully up the hill to their own safe, warm homes. Miranda sat silently in the back-seat, lost in thought.

Miranda tried to keep up her usual cheerful banter as she helped her father wash the dishes, but the effort exhausted her. Her mind was whirling with memories, fragments of conversations, half-formed notions that might mean every-thing—or nothing at all. She hoped he didn't notice. Finally they finished and she hung up the towel, then wandered off to look for Abby. She found her drooping over the piano keyboard, pale hair hanging limply down her back. Miranda touched her shoulder. "Listen, I think I've figured it out. The reason why the phoenix linked us together. How I'm meant to help you, I mean."

She was disappointed that Abby's expression remained glum. "I'll always be a—a phoenix," Abby muttered. "Never a normal person."

"No, listen to me," said Miranda. "How often do you go back to the ruin?"

"You mean, how many times a day?"

"You mean you go back *that* often?"

"Well, yes. I can't stop myself." Abby's hands moved over the piano keys, playing soft chords.

Miranda suspected that Abby's need to return to the ruin was very much like an addiction to a drug—and every bit as dangerous. "So you've never tried to live like a normal person at all."

"What do you mean? What are you talking about?" Abby stopped playing the piano and clasped her hands together.

"You keep going back. You've traveled through time every day for three hundred years!

Regular people don't do that, Abby." She remembered what Mrs. Wainwright had said about people having no choice—they just had to live their lives, day to day. "Listen, Abby. This is the way I can help you." And she searched for the right words to explain.

Abby had Willow's gift and so was magically saved from death. Moved ahead in time, given another chance to live—but with one magical ability. She could choose to return to the place where she died. She had the choice: to live in her new present, or to go back and be a ghost. "Do you see what I mean?" asked Miranda. "It's your choice. But you miss your family and William so much, you haven't been able to accept Willow's gift properly. And I bet that's why you've never grown up in all this time."

"Are you trying to say that all my problems are in my head?" Abby's voice came out a yelp. "That all this time, if I had wanted *not* to be a ghost, I just had to stop going back to the ruin?"

"Maybe *wanting* to go back is normal," Miranda mused. "But maybe actually *going* back is the problem. Everybody misses people who have died. But they just have to carry on with their own lives. In the present." She shook her dark curls. "I know, it sounds too simple.

But I think it's right." She felt shivery with the excitement of her theory. The phoenix had been a gift of new life, but would never work properly unless Abby accepted the new and did not return to the old.

Abby fumbled in her back pocket and withdrew the statue. "So if I choose to live," she said very slowly, turning the figure over in her palm, "then that means I must never ever, *ever* go back to my own time again?"

Miranda remained silent.

"But that would be so hard." Abby shook her head. "You have no idea."

"Going back is hard on you, anyway."

"I hate being a ghost," Abby murmured.

"And here you're *not* a ghost, don't you see?" Miranda clenched her fists in frustration. "It's only in 1693 that you're a ghost. And you've haunted that ruin for years and years and years." She caught her breath. "Abby! Maybe that's why the vacant lot next to the Prindle House is said to be haunted. It's haunted by *you!*"

Abby closed her eyes.

"It's why the phoenix linked us up," Miranda said. "It isn't what we thought. I'm not supposed to change the past at all. But maybe I can help you change your future."

"But you can't keep me from going back," Abby objected. "I can be gone in a second."

"Willpower," said Miranda succinctly. "I can help you remember why you don't want to go back. Why you want to choose life. Come on, promise me now. Promise you will never, ever go back to the ruin again."

Abby sighed. "Oh, Mandy. Choosing life means going on and on and on. That isn't real, either. It isn't normal."

"But if you stop being a ghost at the ruin, I think you'll grow up at last."

"How?" Abby's voice rose eagerly.

Miranda smiled cagily, suddenly happy. "Just promise not to go back. Okay? For at least a week or two. Then we'll know."

"You mean we'll have to wait and see if I grow up, right? But that will take a long time—years and years. More than a few weeks."

Miranda's grin was true and friendly. "Just wait."

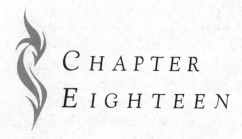

CHAPTER EIGHTEEN

MIRANDA WATCHED ABBY carefully over the next week, but the two girls did not talk much. Abby threw herself into her piano playing—but now, surprisingly, Miranda found it did not bring on headaches anymore. The music poured through the house, music from many eras, telling Abby's story though she herself remained silent. When Abby stopped, Miranda got out her flute, badly neglected since Abby moved in, and practiced her pieces for the spring concert. One evening after dinner, while everyone was still in the big kitchen loading the dishwasher and wiping off countertops, Helen and Philip remarked on the calm.

"Or maybe it's not accurate to call it calm here," mused Helen, cocking her eyebrow at the girls. "Not calm, as in 'settled.'"

"More like 'the calm before the storm'?" Philip asked.

"Exactly," confirmed Helen. "Well, girls? What's going on? All this sweetness and light is making me nervous."

"I feel like we're waiting for something to happen," added Philip.

Miranda bit her lip and scrubbed the stove top extra hard. Abby shrugged her shoulders as she put containers of food in the refrigerator.

"Well, whatever it is," Philip said as he and Helen left the kitchen, cups of tea in hand, "I hope the weather holds."

When they were alone, Abby turned to Miranda. "I don't know why," she began with a tentative smile, "but it's been easier, somehow, living with you lately. I—I could get used to it."

Miranda knew that her answer could change the course of Abby's life. It was an awesome responsibility. "It's nice," she agreed carefully. "Now that we're not fighting every second."

Abby's pale face was as serious as Miranda's own. "You know, a lot of the bad stuff was my fault." She put away the last pot and leaned against the cupboard. "I wasn't giving anyone a chance. It's like you said. I've never been happy because I've always been so tied to the past. Lots of times I've stayed with nice families—or had good situations where I was welcome—but whenever I especially like a family or a place, I seem to get meaner than ever. Partly it's because I know I can't stay long, because I can't give them an explanation for why I never change or grow. And partly because I know I'll hurt them when I leave so suddenly. I find myself acting really rotten so that they'll *want* me to leave. It's easier to go," she said ruefully, "when no one wants you to stay."

"But I do understand why you don't grow. And I bet my parents will, too, when you tell them your story."

"I'm not telling them. And I don't want you to, either. Not yet, anyway." Abby wiped off the table with a damp sponge, then rinsed it out in the sink. "This is the longest time I've ever stayed away from the ruin, you know? I'm doing it for you. To test your theory." She wiped her hands on the dish towel and hung it neatly on the rack. "But I still don't see how you'll know whether I'm growing in only a couple weeks."

"But you promised me you'd wait. You promised!"

"I know, I know. I'm trying my hardest. But if your theory is wrong, and I can't grow up after all, do you think maybe—maybe I can still stay with your family a while? I guess then we'd have to tell your parents the truth—but I bet they'd never believe it."

"Face it, Abby, they'd *have* to believe you if you lived here for ten years and still looked exactly the same." *Ten years? Do I really want her here that long?*

"I guess you're right. Do you think they'd cover for me?"

"Cover for you?" asked Miranda, puzzled.

"Well, yes. They'd have to hide me from the rest of the people in Garnet, or else help me find a place to stay somewhere else. You'll be grown up, and there I'll be."

"I know they'd help you all they could." Miranda had a brief flash into a distant future when she herself was grown up and had children. She would bring her children here to visit their grandparents, and there would be Abby, still thirteen-pretending-to-be-fifteen, still with long, pale hair, blue jeans, a smirky smile, leafing through all her old photographs or pounding the piano keys . . . unchanged. It was a dreadful thought, and she pushed the vision away. "I think you might be able to stay a while longer," was all she said. "I've been thinking about it."

———

Susannah took Miranda aside after their gym class later that week. "It seems like I never see you anymore since Abby moved in. Are you going crazy? I know I would be."

"Things are getting better." Miranda hesitated. She had not told her friend anything at all about Abby's real predicament, nor would she, though sometimes the secret was hard to hold in.

"It's really weird," Susannah continued. "Abby was such a *disaster,* but now she's being really friendly. Totally Jekyll and Hyde. How about coming over today after school, both of you? It'll give us a chance to catch up with each other, and Nonny is still going on about how much Abby's picture in the newspaper looks like that girl she knew so many years ago. I think she'd get a kick out of meeting Abby. She's really tied to the past. Comes from being so old, I guess."

For a second Miranda felt confused. *How can Sue know Abby's secret?* Then she realized her friend was talking about Nonny. "Sounds fun," she said. "Let's ask Abby."

The three girls walked to Susannah's house together and headed straight for the kitchen. Nonny sat at the table, her arm in a cast resting on the tabletop as she tore lettuce leaves with her crooked fingers.

"Hiya, Nonny," said Susannah. She walked around the table and kissed her great-grand-mother. "Put your glasses on and look who I've brought to see you."

The old woman fumbled for the glasses that dangled on a fine gold chain about her neck. She perched them on her nose and peered at Miranda. "Hello, Mandy, dear." Then she looked at Abby. "Oh, my, you're the girl from the newspaper photo!"

Abby stared back, spots of red staining her pale cheeks. "Hello, Mrs. Johnston."

"I can't tell you, child, how much you re-semble a student I had once. Years ago—oh, *decades* ago now. You're the spitting image. My stars, it's like seeing a ghost."

Abby murmured a polite response. Susan-nah and Miranda left them alone while they collected the things needed for brownies: mix-ing bowl, spoons, milk, egg, chocolate, flour, sugar. . . . Miranda brought the ingredients to the table where Nonny was leaning toward Abby.

"It seems like only yesterday I was a young teacher," Nonny was saying. "And now here I am, older than the hills." She laughed merrily. "Time just flies, doesn't it?"

"Yes, it does." Abby nodded solemnly. "Whether you're having fun—or not."

Was time flying yet for Abby? Miranda, still holding the mixing bowl, looked at Abby with appraising eyes. If only her hunch were right . . .

They should know any day now.

"Any day now" turned out to be the very next day. Another snowy Saturday morning and Dan's happy voice in the kitchen brought a sleepy Miranda downstairs quickly. He was sitting with Abby and Helen at the kitchen table, eating stacks of pancakes.

"Mmm!" he greeted her, mouth full. "Lazybones don't git no pancakes."

"Can you believe this weather?" asked Abby. "This is unreal, all this snow. I don't remember a winter like this since—" She broke off, glancing at Helen. "Well, in years."

Miranda laughed. "Years and years and years, perhaps?"

Helen looked puzzled. She slipped a plate of warm pancakes onto the table at Miranda's place. "Well, you three can stay cozy and have fun. But it's business as usual for me. I wish babies took days off for snow." She kissed Miranda and Abby before shrugging on her coat and calling good-bye up the stairs to Philip.

After she left, the kitchen was enveloped in

a deep calm. Dan picked up the newspaper and turned to the sports section. Abby carried the empty plates to the sink and began washing up. Miranda watched the heavy flakes fly past the window over the sink, and she thought for a moment she heard a bird's song faintly from the tree outside, but then all was still again. She felt the snow had been falling forever. Suddenly the silence was broken by a shriek from Abby as a steel knife she had cleaned and dried slipped out of her hands. It nicked her foot as it dropped to the floor.

"Oww, oww!" yelped Abby, hopping around the kitchen on her uninjured foot. "I'll never walk again!"

"Melodrama." Dan grinned, pulling her into the nearest chair. "Take your sock off and let's see if you're going to bleed to death."

"Don't stain the linoleum, whatever you do," teased Miranda. "Bloodstains are *so* hard to get out."

Abby glowered at them both, but stripped off her sock and held her foot up. The cut was no more than a scratch, and Miranda's eyes brushed over it, caught instead by a far more riveting sight.

"Look," she breathed, grabbing Abby's foot in both hands.

"Ouch!" protested Abby. "What are you doing?"

"Don't move the patient," cautioned Dan, crouching at her side. "She may go into shock."

"Oh, cut it out." Abby attempted to pull her foot from Miranda's grasp. "Lay off me, you two. I guess I'll recover after all."

"Look!"

Both Dan and Abby stared at Miranda, then down at Abby's foot.

"What is it?" asked Abby.

"Your foot, Abby. Look."

"That's just a scratch," said Dan. He stood up. "You'll live, won't you, poor girl?"

"No, Dan, *look*." Miranda pointed to Abby's toe, to the toe that had been bruised for three hundred years.

"Oh my God," murmured Abby. It sounded like a prayer.

"I don't get it." Dan stared at Abby's foot, perplexed. "What are you talking about? It's just an ordinary toe. A little knobbier than most, maybe, but—"

"But a toe," breathed Abby, "without a bruise."

Miranda's eyes locked with Abby's in wonderment. "You know what this means?"

"It means somehow I've *changed*." She

leapt up and wrapped her arms around Miranda. "But I *never* change."

"How long now since you've been back to the ruin?"

"I don't get it," muttered Dan. "What are you talking about?"

"I told you. I had a theory that she had to stay in the present. She had to accept the gift of the phoenix in order to grow." Miranda examined Abby's toe again. "And I was right!"

"It's been twelve days," Abby told them, her voice shrill with excitement. "No—wait, maybe thirteen? Going on two weeks." Right then and there, Abby undid the button on her jeans, unzipped them and stepped out, flinging them onto a kitchen chair.

Dan gaped at her. "What are you—?"

But Miranda knew, and leaned over to peer at Abby's thigh.

"Oh, Mandy, Mandy, look. Is it really true?" asked Abby, her voice trembling.

And to Miranda's eyes it did seem that the narrow scarlet burn had faded and grown smaller. The skin around the edges was light pink now, not angry red, as if new skin were trying to grow. She nodded. "It's true."

Abby sank wordlessly into a chair.

Miranda handed her back the blue jeans.

"You're growing now," she said matter-of-factly. "Changing and growing, just like everybody else." She struggled to keep her voice under control, but she wanted to yell it to the treetops, scattering the snow. Her theory had been right. Abby could *live*.

Dan collapsed into a chair. "This is amazing. What happens now?"

Abby shrugged, still staring at her bruiseless toe and healing burn. But Miranda spoke confidently. "Now comes the hard part. If it's staying in the present that lets you grow, you have to be sure never, ever to go back. No one else gets to escape to another time when the present is bad news. Why should you? If you want to be real, you have to stick around and deal with it."

"Simple as that, huh?" muttered Dan.

Miranda shook her head, eyes on Abby. "Probably the hardest thing you will ever have to do." She placed a hand on Abby's knee. "But it might be worth it in the end."

"When is the end?" Abby's voice was a whisper.

"Well—"

"When I die, right?"

Miranda was silent. Choosing life meant choosing death, but at least a death not by her own hand. Life and death—each was a part of the other, part of a cycle that no one could avoid. And yet the phoenix had given Abby the chance to choose. She could be a ghost and exist on and on forever—or she could be a real person and grow and change and, yes, eventually die, just like every other person in the world. But choosing would not be easy, even so. *What would I choose?* Miranda asked herself and was surprised when she could not answer that question right away.

But Abby had had a much longer time to dwell on the meaning of eternal existence. She raised her head and smiled at Miranda and Dan, and Miranda saw tears in the corners of her eyes. "It is simple, after all," Abby murmured. "Even if it does mean I can never go back. I'll go crazy if I have to be stuck for even one more second. I *want* to grow up. I *want* to become an old lady—I *want* to become wise!" She grinned at them tremulously through her tears and brushed her pale hair back over her shoulders. "And when I do die—," she hesitated. "When I'm very old and die at last, maybe *then* I'll see my family again—and William, too."

"Probably you will," said Miranda softly. "Probably they will have been waiting."

Dan went home for lunch, promising to return in the late afternoon. Miranda and Abby donned their boots and skidded down the hill into town. While Miranda had a flute lesson with Mrs. Wainwright, Abby trudged purposefully through the drifts around the common to the stationery store on Main Street. When she returned at the end of Miranda's lesson, she carried a bulky plastic bag.

"Nice to see you again," said Mrs. Wainwright, shaking Abby's thin hand. She turned Abby's hand over in her own. "You have strong fingers, my dear. Do you play the piano?"

"A bit," Abby admitted.

"Does she ever," said Miranda. "She's played for many years."

Mrs. Wainwright looked at Abby appraisingly. "Are you interested in auditioning to play in the spring concert? We have room on the program for one more performer."

Abby started to shake her head, then stopped. A hesitant smile broke across her face. "Yes, I'd like to," she said. "Very much."

"Then let's set up a time for you to come play for me after school, and we'll see what we can do." Mrs. Wainwright went to get her calendar.

"It's been so long since I've felt like throwing myself into things," Abby whispered to Miranda as they waited for the music teacher. "I've almost forgotten how to say yes to something."

After arrangements had been made for Abby's audition, the two girls headed back up the hill. Abby opened her plastic bag to show Miranda her purchase: two large photograph albums bought with the allowance Philip and Helen gave her. "It's time to start filing some things away, I think," she said, and when they arrived at the house she set straight to work. She spent the rest of the afternoon organizing her old pictures into the pages.

Miranda sat in her window seat and tried to read. She listened to the grind of the snowplows clearing the street. It was a welcome sound, the sound of a town, paralyzed by yet another snowfall, coming back to life. She closed her book and walked down the hall to Abby's room.

"Come in."

Miranda peered around the door. Abby's beaded satchel lay open on the bed. She was sorting through her belongings, placing some carefully on the pillow to keep, tossing others aside. The phoenix lay at the foot of the bed on the folded quilt.

"Hey, don't forget your old pal."

Abby shook her head. "I don't want it anymore." She went to sit at her desk and picked up a brittle-edged photograph. She pulled back the clear plastic cover of an album page and centered the picture. Pressing the plastic film firmly down, she spoke quietly. "*This* is my time now. Is has to be. If I'm never going back to 1693, then I must stop thinking about it. Having that bird around will always remind me . . . of what I've lost. Having it around is like what a bottle of vodka is to a recovering alcoholic. Unnecessary temptation."

"But it was Willow's gift to you."

Abby shrugged. "Leave it on the bed. I'll do something with it."

"You could always *give* it to someone, I suppose."

Abby looked up at her. "Do you really still want it, Mandy? If you do, you may have it. But watch out."

"Oh, come on! That statue saved your life!"

"And maybe it would save your life one day, too, in the same way. Think about it."

Miranda turned the little figure over. The cold stone bird lay in her palm as if in a nest.

Dan tipped Miranda into their snow fort in the Brownes' side yard, and then tumbled in on top of her. "I've got you now, my beauty," he laughed evilly.

She squealed as the snow touched the unprotected back of her neck, and she reached up to stuff a fistful of snow down his coat.

Dan caught her wrist and held it away from him. She struggled to get him off her, overpower him, and wash his face with the fresh snow, but he was too strong. They wrestled happily for some minutes before Miranda sighed and relaxed under him. He bent his head to kiss her, and his lips were surprisingly warm.

They smiled at each other. "Peace?" he asked.

"Peace," she agreed, and he rolled off her. She sat up and leaned against him, their backs pressed against the hard wall of the snow fort.

"This is a good place to be," he said. "I wouldn't want to be anywhere else."

"Me, neither." She snuggled closer.

They sat there like that for a long time, not talking. Miranda found the quiet cold healing, soothing. Everything lately had been so strange, so unfathomable. She hoped now that Abby was indeed growing again, her own life might become less complicated. How nice it would be to have nothing more to concentrate on than Dan's nearness, their special love. Soon she would be able to relax with him, content in the knowledge that there was nothing else more vital to her. But before she could put the problems with Abby behind her, there was something else she needed to do.

"Will you stay for dinner?" she asked Dan.

He hugged her. "Love to."

And so it was after dinner that the three Brownes and Abby and Dan were gathered by the living room fire. Although she usually stayed well away from fires, tonight Abby made a point of sitting next to Miranda and Dan right in front of the screen. Together they watched the sparks.

Helen and Philip looked up when Miranda turned to them and cleared her throat.

"I want to talk to you guys."

"Okay, shoot," said Philip, closing his book. Helen placed a slip of paper in hers to mark the place and laid the book on the coffee table. They looked at Miranda expectantly.

"I would like to change my mind," she began, her eyes on Abby, who was watching the flames dance as if mesmerized. "I mean, about Abby."

Abby turned abruptly to Miranda, the spell broken. Her eyes were bright.

"I know there have been—umm—problems," Miranda said. The fire at her back warmed her with a heat that spread to flush her face. She licked her lips, suddenly nervous, but knew her words were the right ones now. "A lot of problems. But I think we've worked things out. The social worker said that Abby could stay through March—but that's almost here. So I think we should do something legal—something so she can stay longer."

"How much longer did you have in mind?" asked Helen carefully.

"Like about fifty years."

Philip whooped, then leapt off the couch to hug Miranda. He reached over and hugged Abby, too. "I think the best we can do is get permission to keep you until you're eighteen, Abby. Will that be long enough for you?"

"You'd always be part of the family, even after that," Helen hastened to add. "But legally you would only have to stay until you turn eighteen."

"Have to stay," murmured Abby. "Have to? It sounds like a prison sentence. I would absolutely *love* to stay. Till I'm eighteen—or longer."

"Like forever," said Miranda.

"Fortunately not that long—anymore." Abby and Miranda exchanged a long, intimate look that left Helen and Philip puzzled.

"I have the sneaking suspicion there is something I'm not in on," said Helen.

"I feel that, too," said Philip. "Girls? Dan?"

"Abby sure has a story to tell—," he began, but broke off when Abby shook her head.

"But not now," Abby said. "Not yet."

"But sometime," Miranda said.

"It's an illustrated story," added Dan. "Kind of like a photo essay."

Abby caught her breath, but Miranda and Dan smiled at her reassuringly. They would not tell Abby's story or show Abby's collection of photographs until she was ready. But it was a story that should be told, Miranda thought. It was a story like no other.

"Well, if we're not having stories," said Philip, "how about having hot chocolate?"

"A toast to Abby," said Helen, getting to her feet.

"Hot chocolate—with whipped cream to celebrate!" Philip followed Helen out of the room. "Just make mine nonfat." Their happy voices filtered back from the kitchen.

When they had gone, Miranda tugged the stone phoenix from her jeans pocket. She held it out to Abby.

"I gave it to you freely, Mandy," said Abby. "Keep it if you really want it."

How to decide? A wealth of conflicting emotions glistened in Miranda's eyes as she stared down at the small stone whistle that had saved Abby's life and at the same time held her captive for three hundred years. Is it possible simply to refuse magic?

Finally she pressed the statue into Abby's hand. "No, I don't need it," she said firmly, and knew it was true.

"If I had known what Willow was really giving me that day, would I have accepted her gift?" Abby shrugged, gazing directly at Miranda as if searching for something in the other girl's eyes. "Maybe—who knows? I wouldn't have wanted to have missed . . . all this. Your parents—and you, Mandy."

Abby's pale eyes mirrored the white stone of the bird. "A phoenix," she murmured. "Just a cold stone whistle." She ran her fingertips almost lovingly over the surface of the figure. "A bird, that's all." She raised her head and looked around the Brownes' comfortable living room—a warm, inviting room in an old New England house in a small New England town now well into the last years of the twentieth century—and then turned to Miranda and Dan. In the depths of those eyes Miranda caught a last glimpse of the young Puritan girl Abby had once been.

Abby held the phoenix high. Miranda watched, transfixed, suddenly knowing what her friend was going to do.

"Thank you," Abby whispered to it almost inaudibly and with one sharp movement, tossed the stone whistle into the fire.

Neither Miranda nor Dan tried to stop her, though the small explosion that followed brought Helen and Philip running in from the kitchen. As they all watched, sparks shot high into the chimney with a roaring, wind-filled blast. A high-pitched screech hung in the air before fading to a long, clear note—a mere whisper of song. Then the song, with the sparks, disappeared, and only the embers were left, and the people, and the comforting hot chocolate, inviting them to drink.